Box Camera Chronicles

Box Camera Chronicles

❀

Stories of the 20ᵗʰ Century

Pearl Atkins Schwartz

iUniverse, Inc.
New York Lincoln Shanghai

Box Camera Chronicles
Stories of the 20ᵗʰ Century

iUniverse books may be ordered through booksellers or by contacting:

iUniverse
2021 Pine Lake Road, Suite 100
Lincoln, NE 68512
www.iuniverse.com
1-800-Authors (1-800-288-4677)

ISBN-13: 978-0-595-37110-5 (pbk)
ISBN-13: 978-0-595-81510-4 (ebk)
ISBN-10: 0-595-37110-8 (pbk)
ISBN-10: 0-595-81510-3 (ebk)

Printed in the United States of America

To my children and grandchildren who
enrich every minute of my life,
And to Jules who provides the laughs.

Contents

❁

ACKNOWLEDGEMENTS

I want to thank my friend and teacher, Mary Webb whose constant encouragement gave me impetus; my friend, Sue Clark, who took a chance on me; and my buddies, Patricia Mills, Janet Oman, and Carla Thornton, who always raised the bar and hauled me over the top.

She waited a few seconds. "Yeah," she called down from the landing.

Saturday arrived. Wild emotions thrashed around in Bessie all day. Her cheeks flushed in waves. Her shoulders and arms twitched.

While drying the dishes after supper, her eyes followed her mother's every move in the kitchen. She watched for the start of the Saturday night routine as her mother prepared to go to play Bingo and her father to his pinochle game. At last, her father, who was reading at the kitchen table, folded his newspaper, put on his jacket and felt in his pockets for his cigarettes and keys. "I'm going, Sarah," he called to Bessie's mother. "Goodnight, Bessie. Go to sleep early."

Bessie stood in the doorway of the bedroom and watched her mother change her dress. In the closet, Bessie spotted the box with the silver shoes her mother had worn last year to cousin Sylvia's wedding. The silk stockings, she knew, were rolled up in a ball in one of the shoes. Her mother's dress with the silver beads hung on a special hanger next to her father's blue suit.

"You didn't eat much for supper, Bessie," her mother said. "What's the matter? You don't feel good? Maybe you need a bicarbonate?"

"No, Mama. I feel good."

Her mother gathered her Bingo paraphernalia in a black tote bag. Bessie looked at the kitchen clock and frowned. That business with the big hand and the little hand of the clock confounded her.

"What time is it, Mama?" she said as her mother was leaving.

"It's ten minutes to eight. Turn on the radio. In ten minutes Fred Allen will be on. Don't stay up to hear the 'Witch's Tale,' you hear? Go to sleep early. You hear, Bessie? Lock the door."

"G'night, Mama."

As soon as the door closed, Bessie rushed to the bedroom. She took her mother's beaded dress from the closet, held it against her body, and looked in the mirror over the dresser. I'll be beautiful, she thought. Everybody will see how nice I look. She put the dress on, kicking her discarded clothes under the bed. The back zipper closed up to her waist and would go no further. She found a safety pin in her mother's sewing box and fastened the dress at the back of the neck. That's all right, she thought. I'll wear my sweater so they won't see my brassiere.

Now the shoes. She opened the box and ran her fingers across the shiny leather. She put the stockings on, tugging at the seams. She twisted and pulled until a hole appeared and a fat run crept up one stocking toward her knee. She found a pair of her mother's circular garters on the bathroom doorknob. The shoes were stiff and pinched her toes as she balanced herself on the heels. She hobbled around the living room a few times, enjoying the sound of the heels on the linoleum floor.

Her mother's lipstick and rouge were in the mirrored medicine cabinet. Leaning over the sink, she drew a curvy red mouth with the lipstick and two circles of rouge on her cheeks.

In one of the dresser drawers she found the "Evening in Paris" bottle in its white satin compartment in the original box. She opened the cologne and poured some into the dress and giggled as the liquid slid down between her breasts.

The familiar radio commercial came on. Soon it would be eight o'clock. Manny would be waiting for her. Manny…

On the street, Bessie hurried toward Goodman's corner, through the fading summer light and the golden spread of the street lamps. She ignored the quizzical looks of the neighbors who sat on their folding chairs along the brick sides of the buildings. As she approached Goodman's corner, her heart sank. She didn't see Manny. There were about eight kids around the milk box, but he was not there. Then one of the girls spotted her.

"Hey, Bessie, Wow! Where'd you get that dress? Hey everybody, get a load of Bessie."

One of the boys crowed, "Bessie, you're gorgeous!"

Bessie blushed and allowed a small smile. She took a deep breath. "Where's Manny?"

Anthony stepped out of the group and, taking her arm, led her toward the curb.

"Manny told me to tell you to meet him in his father's store. He's waiting there for you."

Bessie looked across the street at the glass front of Delgado's Dry Cleaning. A broad window shade covered the inside expanse of glass. "It's closed," she said.

"I know," Anthony said. "But Manny got his father's key and he's in there, waiting for you."

"It's dark," Bessie said.

Anthony started to pull her across the street, but she resisted.

"It's too dark," Bessie said. "I'm afraid to go there."

"Don't be afraid. I tell you, he's waiting there for you. When you go inside he'll put the lights on."

She glanced back at the crowd at the milk box. They were all watching.

Anthony coaxed and chided her across the street to the door of the shop. He pressed the latch and pushed her inside, closing the door behind her.

She stood in the darkness, her heart racing. She did not move, except for her eyes as she scanned every side of the room. She turned to face the sewing machine in the corner. She imagined she could see Mr. Delgado in the shadows working at his machine, a menacing kerchlunk of the treadle almost audible in the darkness.

"Manny," she called in a loud whisper. There was no answer. She stepped closer to the counter and peered into the back of the store. All the clothes hung in white paper sheaths beneath a row of fedora hats on a shelf, looking like white-clad people stand-ing in rows. Something moved.

"Manny," she said aloud. She heard a rustle from the back of the store and stepped backward toward the door.

In a flash, the lights came on. She covered her eyes with the backs of her hands.

"Hi, Bessie!" It was Manny, standing behind the counter.

The rows of clothing opened, and Eddie and Mitch emerged from between the hanging garments.

"Hey, Bessie," Eddie said. "Are you ready for your date with Manny?" He laughed. "I told you he'd meet you."

Bessie stood still, her mouth open. Manny's lips parted in a weak smile. For a moment they all stood in silence.

Then Manny said, "Are you ready?" He stepped out in front of the counter holding a towel around his waist. In a flash, he opened the towel and thrust his naked pelvis forward.

Bessie heard a scream that seemed to come from far away. It was like when she was dreaming and the cry was an echo in her throat. She shut her eyes, closing out the vision of Manny's long brown thighs and that thing dangling between them.

Eddie and Mitch doubled over laughing. Then, Manny did a crazy jig as he came toward her.

She fumbled with the door and found herself outside, run-ning and stumbling toward home. The laughs and screeches from Goodman's corner rang in her ears. She ran with her arms stretched before her, reaching for something—anything solid. She stumbled and fell onto the pavement. One of her mother's silver shoes bounced on the sidewalk and fell into the gutter.

"Hey, Cinderella," somebody called. "You lost your slipper!"

Bessie ran until she could no longer hear their laughter, until she felt the great iron door of her building close behind her. She stumbled up the steps. "You shouldn'ta done that, Manny." Her sobs echoed in the stairwell. She leaned against the door of her flat, clutching her mother's beaded dress with one hand and wiping the red color from her lips with the other. "I don't like you no more, Manny. I don't like you no more."

WING-TIPS

Granny Serafina told him that envy is a hot ball of fire that bounces up from hell to burn a man's flesh. Jesús took those frightening words to heart, but as much as he tried, he could not beat back his searing desire for his brother's magnificent brown and white wing-tip shoes.

Jesús knew Diego had won one hundred pesos at the cockfights and spent fifty of them for the shoes, bought new from a big shop in Mexico City instead of the second-hand market where the family got its clothes. Their father had looked at the shoes with suspicion when Diego brought them home, but his attitude softened when Diego gave Papa the fifty pesos he had left from his winnings.

Now, there they were in plain view on a shelf over their bed where the shoes shared space with a painted plaster of paris figure of the Virgin of Guadalupe. Jesús knew his brother kept the shoes there to taunt him.

Each night, when Diego came home from work, he took the shoes off the shelf, put them on, tied the laces with a flourish, and walked around the room twice, smirking at Jesús who watched from the kitchen table. Then Diego would remove the shoes and place them back on the shelf, adjusting their position to perfect symmetry.

"Diego, when are you going to wear your precious shoes?" Jesús said after two weeks of watching his brother perform his daily ritual.

"It's no business of yours," Diego answered. "And keep your hands off. If you touch them, I will know. I have a way of telling."

Jesús did not doubt his brother's words. Indeed, the shoes themselves seemed to radiate magic as they sat in their splendor on the shelf. As soon as Jesús came home from school each day, he went to stare at the shoes. He had no doubt they had certain powers. He convinced himself they had the power to make Laura, the blue-eyed *gringa* who worked in the cafe on the Street of the Bakers, take notice of anyone who would wear them. His heart fluttered every time he thought of her, which was fifty times a day.

There was no other reason to envy Diego. Jesús, at fifteen, was taller and more muscular than his older brother. His skin was fairer, and his black hair was fine and shiny. Diego was ugly, small and dark with a pitted complexion. He had to force his kinky hair down with thick pomade. Diego's nickname in the gang he belonged to was *Rata*. But even though Diego had never gone past third grade in school, he was smart. He had always managed to find work, and now at eighteen he had held down his job in the lamp factory for six months. He always had money in his pocket and kept in Papa's favor by paying for his keep. Diego often gave their sister, Pachita, a few *centavos* to buy sweets.

Jesús knew that even if he saved every *centavo* he earned at his weekend job at the bathhouse, it would take him a year to save enough to buy brown and white wing-tip shoes. By that time, Laura would become someone else's sweetheart. It was torture for him to watch her in the cafe Friday nights as she moved with grace around the tables, serving coffee. She had a way of making up names in *Inglés* for the customers. Guillermo was "Bill," Alberto was "Al," and she called Jesús "Joe." Sometimes she lingered, resting her palms on a table, leaning over just a little to talk to a customer. Jesús would hold his breath, wishing she would do the same when she stopped at his table.

He always came to the cafe alone, hoping Laura would notice him. He wore his one and only white shirt, washed and ironed every Friday for him by his grandmother. But his shoes were a disgrace—sturdy black work boots that Papa bought for himself and his sons every year.

Jesús wanted to ask Laura to the dance held every Sunday night in the Casa Grande courtyard. But, he knew that even if she would agree to go with him, he would be embarrassed in his black boots when Diego showed up in his brown and white wing-tips.

Jesús ran his finger over a scab on his eyebrow and thought of the day Diego had come home early from work and caught him standing on a chair near the shelf. Jesús was staring at the wing-tips with such intensity that he did not hear his brother.

"Ay, you dirty *ladrón*," Diego yelled. "What do you think you're doing?" Without another word, he grabbed the legs of the chair and swept Jesús off, throwing him to the floor. Jesús's head struck the edge of a table and a one-inch gash opened across his eyebrow. Blood poured down his face and seeped into his mouth and stained his shirt. Granny Serafina, who had been dozing in her chair in the kitchen, rushed into the room. She took a broom to Diego who ran, laughing, out of the house.

There had to be a way to get Diego to let Jesús wear the shoes just one time. Jesús got the idea of inviting Diego into the bath-house where there was a hole in the wall of the women's dressing room. But Diego sneered. "Don't be such a fool. Why would I want to see those old women's fat asses? My Rosa lets me see her naked any time I want."

One afternoon Jesús walked home from school, taking a different route in order to buy a lottery ticket from his friend Bustos who lived on the Street of the Tinsmiths.

"What's the matter, *amigo?*" Bustos asked. "You look like a ghost."

"Ay, it's that Laura from the cafe. She's driving me *loco.*"

"What do you mean? You're not her boyfriend, are you?"

"No, but if I could take her to the dance…

"Why don't you ask her?"

"She won't even look at me. She passes my table when I go in for coffee, and she doesn't even notice me." A few seconds passed. "If I could only wear my brother's wing-tip shoes. Ah, they're so grand. They're magic. She would notice me then. If, by some miracle…"

Bustos rubbed his thin mustache with thumb and forefinger. "A miracle? Why don't you try *la curandera?*"

"Ugh! What can that old witch do? I'm afraid to even think of her with all those stinking herbs and candles."

"Well, I know for sure that last year she was able to raise an erection on old Pancho, the nightwatchman in the bakery. Now, he and his wife have twin boys."

Jesús stared at his friend. "But what can she do to make Laura love me?"

"She can do anything. Once she got mad at a customer who wouldn't pay for a love potion she gave him. She cast a spell on him. Now he's bald as a newborn mouse."

Jesús took his lottery ticket and walked to the Casa Grande all the while thinking of the possibilities. *La curandera* lived on the Street of the Bakers. He had passed her place many times, and even though there were no windows in her room, he could smell her nasty potions on the street.

After his evening meal, he went to the back door of the tavern on the street and learned from the local gangleader that his lottery ticket was a loser. He put the useless ticket into his pants pocket and walked home. He decided he would go to see the sorceress the next day.

The smell outside the red door of the sorceress was worse than he'd remembered. He knocked, then waited a full three minutes before the old hag let him in. The room was dark as night in contrast to the bright afternoon sun outside. He could make out a deep smoking kettle on the iron stove and five long shelves on one wall holding jars filled with what he imagined to be herbs. He stood at the closed door until he heard the woman mumbling. She was seated at a square wooden table in the middle of the room. He had to move closer to make out what she was saying. "What do you want?" she rasped.

His nose was running, and his eyes stung from the fumes rising from the kettle. "I have some trouble. I think you can help me". He wiped his nose with his sleeve.

"Well, speak up. What's your trouble?"

Well, you see, there's this *gringa* who works in the cafe. She is *muy linda*. But, she doesn't care for me. Could you...I mean do you have a potion that will make her love me?"

The woman snickered. "I have such a potion." She shook her head up and down. "It will cost you twelve pesos."

"Twelve pesos...that is too much money." Jesús felt an ache in his stomach. "I have only six pesos."

"Hah! What do you expect to get for six pesos?"

Jesús swallowed hard. "Well, maybe if I had the shoes...she would go with me to the dance."

"Shoes? What shoes? I have no time for this garbage."

"Well, you see, my brother, Diego, he has these shoes..." Jesús told the hag about his passion for the wing-tips. When he finished, he looked up. His vision had adjusted to the darkness and he forced himself to look into her crossed eyes. Every other tooth in the upper row of her mouth was missing. A thin spread of stringy black hair escaped from a red bandana that covered her forehead.

"Pssh," she expelled through her teeth. She looked at him for a full minute until he started to back away toward the door. "It will cost you six pesos. Come tomorrow. Bring me two goose eggs and a cup of sugar water."

Jesús ran all the way back to his house. Where would he get goose eggs? And if he knew where to get them, how would he get them by tomorrow?

When he arrived home his sister, Pachita, was pleading with their father to let her go to the dance on Sunday. Diego, already finished with his meal, was wiping his plate with a tortilla.

"Ah, let her go, Papa," Diego said. "Fourteen is old enough for her to go. There are younger girls at the dance, lots of them."

Their father looked at Pachita, who was hopping from one foot to the other in anticipation. "All right. She can go," he said, "but only if you, Diego, will be responsible for her." Pachita threw her arms around Diego's neck and kissed him. "By that, I mean," Papa continued, "you will be by her side every minute, and she is not to dance with any of your filthy *cuadrilla* friends. And you will bring her home not later than eleven o'clock. Understood?"

Diego nodded without enthusiasm.

The next day, Jesús took two brown chicken eggs from Granny's basket and poured some water from the kettle into a jar with a large spoonful of sugar. He carried them in his hat which he held under his arm when he left for school, but he did not go to school for fear that the eggs would be smashed. Instead, he went to the market hoping to find goose eggs. At two o'clock, he left the market and turned down the Street of the Bakers. He stood outside the red door and forced himself to knock. The old hag grabbed his elbow and pulled him into the foul-smelling room.

"Did you bring the money?" she said.

He held out the six coins which she took and put into a jar.

"And the goose eggs?"

He gave her the brown chicken eggs. "*Bufón*...These are not goose eggs. What are you trying to pull?"

"I know. I couldn't find goose eggs in the market. Please take these eggs. They're fresh from my own Aunt Graciela's hen."

"I need goose eggs."

Jesús broke out in a sweat. He put his hand into his pants pocket. "Look, I can give you this lottery ticket. I bought it just this morning. It's probably a winner, but I'll give it to you. The prize is a golden wristwatch."

The sorceress took the ticket and held it close to the flames from the stove, pretending to read it. She turned to Jesús.

"Do you think I need your stinking lottery ticket for a wristwatch?" But she put the ticket in her pocket and pointed to a stool near the stove. "Sit down. Where is the sugar water?" He retrieved the jar from the hat. "Take off your shoes," she commanded.

The sorceress took the jar of sugar water and intoned some unintelligible words over the kettle bubbling on the stove. She threw the sugar water into the kettle which emitted a blast of steam. From three copper cups on the table, she took red, green and yellow powders and mixed them in the cup of her hand. She intoned some words in a sing-song voice and flung the powders into the kettle. Next, she took the eggs and placed each of them on Jesús's feet. When she was satisfied that they would not roll off, she made a circular gesture with her arms over the eggs and closed her eyes.

When the ordeal was over, Jesús went home and lay down at the foot of his bed so that he could see the brown and white wing-tip shoes on the shelf. He was feeling woozy and wondered if he was coming down with a *maldad* of the stomach. He was worried that *la curandera's* spell would not work because of the chicken eggs. Besides, she would find out about the useless lottery ticket. All is lost, he thought. The six pesos, his total savings, were lost, too.

Jesús felt even sicker the next day, Saturday. His Granny made him stay in bed and sent Pachita to the bathhouse to tell the boss that Jesús would not work that day. He lay shivering on the thin mattress, although his head was hot. Granny placed a sour-smelling poultice on his forehead, and Jesús fell in and out of restless sleep all that day. On Sunday, he became aware that Pachita and Diego were preparing to go to the dance. The shoes were gone from the shelf.

At midnight, he was awakened by a commotion in his room. His father was screaming at Diego.

"Where is she? You were to stay by her side. How could you have lost her?" Papa paced the room. "We'll have to go look for her."

Diego took off his shoes and put on his black boots. The wing-tips were left on the floor pointing inward like *la curandera's* eyes. Jesús wondered if this was an omen.

When Diego and Papa came home, Pachita was not with them. Papa began to pace the room. All of a sudden, Papa wrenched his belt from around his waist and began to beat Diego from his head to his feet. Diego ran from the bedroom to the kitchen and back again to escape his father's lashes. Then, he raced out of the house crying and cursing as he ran down the street.

Diego did not come home on Monday, but Pachita did. She stood, meek and silent, in the kitchen, her eyes fixed on her father.

"Where have you been? *Digamé*!" Papa yelled.

Pachita turned and looked out of the open door to the street. Papa followed her gaze. Pedro, the barber's fifteen year old son, was standing at the curb looking in. Papa went to the door with his fists clenched. Pedro turned and disappeared down the street.

"What does this mean?"

"He wants to be my boyfriend," Pachita murmured. Their father's face turned red. Jesús knew he would not beat Pachita. She never gave him reason to be angry with her. Only the boys were forced to suffer his blows when he was mad. Now, Papa seemed not to know how to handle the situation. Pachita and Granny and Papa sat in the kitchen for a long time and talked in low tones. Jesús was still too sick to care.

That evening, a man who worked with Diego in the lamp factory, came to tell Papa that Diego had joined a merchant ship and would not return.

"*Bueno...Adios*," Papa muttered. "Let him see how it is to live among strangers." The rims of his eyes were red. He ate no supper but drank a half bottle of rum and slept all night with his head on the kitchen table.

Jesús was feeling stronger on Tuesday, but Granny made him remain in bed and fed him some clear broth in a cup. "Tomorrow you should have some real food...some bean soup." She placed an extra pillow under his head. He noticed that the wing-tips were back on the shelf. He sat up. The shoes! Now that Diego was gone, the shoes would be his. His heart jumped. That old sorceress. She had done the magic.

Pachita was in school. His father had gone to work. Granny would be going to the market, as she did every day at two o'clock. He watched the minutes and hours pass until Granny left the house with her cloth bag. Then, he took the shoes down.

He sat on the edge of his bed. The shoes were on the floor before him. He picked up the right shoe and put his bare toes in. He pushed, but his foot would go only half way into the shoe. He tried the left foot. It was too small. He went to the kitchen and dipped his hand into the lard pot. He sat on his bed again and rubbed the lard all over his feet. He tried the left shoe again, and then the right. A dark shadow fell over his heart. Diego's brown and white wing-tip shoes were too small.

When Granny came home, Jesús was pacing in the kitchen. "You are better," she cooed. "Look, I have bought a chicken. Tomorrow you will have a real meal. I will make my spicy chicken with beans to put some color in your face." He sat on the bed where Granny and Pachita slept near the stove.

Jesús, with a heavy heart, watched Granny fill a large basin with water and empty a bowl of pink-speckled pinto beans into it. She put the basin on the floor in a corner of the room. Jesús was aware that she was talking to him as she prepared the evening meal of enchilados and fried bananas, but his turmoil drowned out her words. After a while, she came to him and put her hand on his head. "I'm such a foolish old woman," she said. "You need to rest. Go back to bed. I'll bring you some more broth."

That night, Jesús cried into his pillow. He lay all night like a fallen tree unable to move. In the morning, he heard Papa and Granny arguing in the kitchen. "He should go to school tomorrow," Papa said.

"Leave him alone, Ricardo. He needs another day and a good meal in his stomach. Then he will go to school."

After his father left for work on Wednesday, Jesús came into the kitchen and sat in Granny's chair. She glanced at him from time to time.

Jesús watched her as she swept the linoleum toward the basin of beans on the floor. *Caramba*! The beans had absorbed almost all of the water and had swelled to double their size! He caught his breath. An idea developed and grew big like the bulging beans.

Again, Jesús waited until Granny left for the market. She had put the beans to simmer in a great pot. He removed the lid to smell the spicy stew. He could see the beans bouncing and pushing against the sides of the pot. He smiled.

Jesús took the shoes off the shelf and put them on the kitchen table. The raw beans were kept in a large hopsacking bag leaning against the side of the ice-box. He dragged the bag across the floor to the table, relishing the power and promise in their weight. He took the right shoe and scooped the beans into it. Then, he loaded the left shoe. He filled an enamel teapot with water from the sink and poured the water into the shoes. Then he carefully placed them under his bed. He dragged the bag of beans back across the room.

Now he would wait. The beans would do their work to stretch the wing-tip shoes to fit. Jesús lay on his bed and wondered what part *la curandera's* sorcery had played in this fortunate turn of events.

The evening meal was almost festive. After the blessing, Papa acknowledged Jesús's presence at the table by offering him the first plate of food. Pachita squealed with pleasure at the special treat—chicken with beans.

After the meal, Papa set up the checker board on the kitchen table. Jesús sat across from his father and rubbed his hands. He was feeling lucky tonight. But the game did not progress well for Jesús. He was thinking of the beans from supper crowding his stomach and could not concentrate.

"What are you smiling about?" Papa said, taking three of Jesús's checkers in one move. "Ah, let's forget it. This is no game. Maybe you still have the *maldad*. He stood up and took his seat near the radio.

Jesús put the checkers away and went to lie down on his bed. He felt like a giant. The power that lay under his bed seemed to rise up and enter his body. He fell into a deep sleep.

In the morning, he longed to look under the bed to see if anything had happened, but his father lingered long over his coffee.

"What are you waiting for?" his father grumbled. "Do you think you can afford to stay home from school again?"

"No, Papa. I'm going." With a sorrowful glance at his bed, he left the flat.

At two o'clock, Jesús raced out of the classroom almost knocking over several of his classmates. He ran down the street, but as he neared his home, he thought of Diego. He slowed down to a walk. What would happen when Diego came home after his stint on the merchant ship? Another fearful thought struck him. What if *la curandera* was angry with him because of the lottery ticket? What if he would be punished for the sheer wickedness of his envy? He hesitated at the door of the flat.

As soon as he entered the bedroom, he saw the statue of the Virgin lying face down on the shelf over his bed. He picked it up with care and looked into the Virgin's face. Something was there in the pale shadows of the plaster of paris. Was it a look of sadness? Was it reproach? He knew then that his fears were valid.

He went into the kitchen and sat in a chair for several minutes before taking Granny's broom to the bedroom to sweep the shoes from under the bed.

They emerged, side by side, the toes facing him. The brown and white leather uppers of the wing-tips had separated from the soles. The plump beans between the soles and the uppers appeared like so many teeth in a spread of two impish smiles.

When Granny Serafina came home, she stood in the doorway of the bedroom and stared at the broken shoes on the floor. "Oh, my poor boy," she sighed. She looked at Jesús and shook her head. Then she turned and went back outside. Jesús went to the door and saw her rushing toward the market.

When he picked up the shoes, the soggy beans ran out onto the floor and left a trail from the bedroom to the kitchen sink. His heart ached as he worked to clean up the mess.

His father would be sure to see the mutilated shoes, now back on the shelf. Jesús lay on his bed, facing the shoes, alone with his worries.

When Granny returned, she came into the bedroom with a package wrapped in newspaper. She opened the package and got onto the bed. Bracing herself on the wall, she placed the statue on the shelf next to the shoes. She came down off the bed.

"Another saint?" Jesús said.

"Yes. This is our beloved San Augustín who said that envy is a sin from the devil. Let San Augustín stand next to the shoes and let his wisdom cool your burning." She went into the kitchen.

That evening, Granny Serafina ironed Jesús's white shirt so that it would be ready for him to wear on Friday night.

WEAPONS OF WAR

Clara's mind was a dry well. The Fancy Finds Flea Market was a logical place for a jump-start. As a writer, Clara had gathered compelling material in the dusty stalls of the market. She had found keen inspiration in other people's minutiae—vintage clothes, old diaries, sepia photos, bedraggled toys.

She bypassed the tee shirts, the watches, the handbags and drifted to a vendor of used items. The vendor made eye contact with her. A sign on a corrugated cardboard leaning against the carton proclaimed, THIS ENTIRE BOX ONLY $8.00. NO INDIVIDUAL ITEMS.

A dozen stained hard-backed books stood up in the carton with a row of around twenty limp paperbacks. A one-inch stack of postcards tied with brown straw twine and a leaflet of sheet music were wedged in between the books. Jutting up at the end of the carton was an eight by ten oil painting in a scratched gilt wooden frame.

Clara reached into the carton and picked up the painting. It portrayed a brown horse, his head hanging over a white slat fence, his lifeless eyes cast downward. A thumbprint in the dry paint marked the upper left corner of the canvas. That thumbprint. Something stirred in Clara's chest.

The vendor cast her a hopeful look. "Seven dollars for the whole carton," he said.

"Well, all I really want is this painting."

"Can't do it," the vendor said.

Clara placed the painting on top of the carton and started to move away.

"Six dollars. Take the whole lot for six dollars," the vendor called.

A small flush of victory merged with a stab of guilt. "All right," Clara said. She paid him and lugged the booty to her car parked a block away.

In her three room flat, she set her purchases on the floor of the living room and sat down to examine them. She placed the painting next to her on the floor.

The postcards were disappointing—the ink faded, the messages trite—the "Wish you were here" variety.

After a quick scan of the books she pulled out J.D. Salinger's *Catcher in the Rye* from the hard cover selection and consigned all of the others to a Salvation Army box.

Then Clara turned her attention to the painting. She held it up to the light. No artist's signature was visible. It was evident it was the product of an unskilled hand.

The painting set her reaching back in memory to an image of her father working with charcoal on a large pad on the kitchen table in the Brooklyn flat where she had lived as a child. Her father drew depictions of household objects, views of the elevated train that rattled across the street, and endless drawings of an undernourished maple that pushed up in its wire cage from a square hole in the pavement in front of their house. Clara recalled the intensity of her father's frown as he drew pencil sketches of her and her two teenage brothers and friends who grudgingly sat still for him.

His livelihood as a house painter afforded him residual cans of oil paint that he kept on the floor of a closet. Money was scarce, but he had several small tubes of pigment that he mixed with the paint poured into jars from the half-gallon cans.

Clara looked down at the painting in her lap. She ran her finger over the thumbprint in the upper left corner and remembered another picture, a paper print that her father had rescued from a pile of refuse left on the sidewalk by a family who had moved out of the building. He carried the print into the flat. She watched him remove it from its battered mahogany frame and stand it on the window sill, leaning it against the glass.

"What're you doing, Pop?" she had said.

"I'm going to fix this beautiful picture."

He lined up several jars of his paints on the desk alongside the window and proceeded to restore the color in the faded peonies and roses in a blue and white vase. He placed the print, too soon, back in the old frame and left his thumbprint in the upper left corner.

Their home displayed no books on shelves, no plants on the windowsills, no phonograph proffering operas and symphonies. The only music was that of radio commercials from a Philco on a kitchen shelf. Her father's artistic efforts remained hidden in his huge drawing pad or in various drawers around the house. Only the embellished still life with the thumbprint in the upper left corner graced their parlor wall.

As a child, Clara knew that her parents disliked each other. They communicated in surly monosyllables. They never went anywhere together. They never sat at the table together.

Clara did not dwell on the situation. She thought it was like that in every household. She was content with her father's affection for her. She recalled, when she was little, pushing aside his newspaper to climb on his lap, his moist lips on her eyelids as he kissed her eyes, the sour smell of his daily shot of schnapps, the sharp stubble on his face against her cheek.

But by the time Clara was thirteen, the reality of her parents' conflict had set in. She became aware of their weapons of war. Her mother withheld sex and intimacy. Her father withheld money.

One Sunday evening, Clara came into the house to hear them arguing.

"I need a new dress for the holidays," her mother said, her ice-blue eyes flaring, her bleached blonde hair—a neighborhood scandal—rolled up in curlers

"What's the matter with last year's dress? Who are you trying to impress? Sam Winkler, maybe? I see you looking at his window whenever you pass his house. The neighbors are talking about you."

"My dress is five years old. I just need four dollars..

"Well, I haven't got four dollars. You think money grows on trees?"

The next day, with the help of Clara's two brothers, her mother moved Clara's bed out of her bedroom into the parlor next to the boys' pullout sofa. A boarder moved into the small room.

Clara sat on the stoop of the building, a knot of apprehension choking her as waited for her father to come home from work. She stood up and tried to speak as he approached, but he greeted her with a kiss on top of her head and rushed into the house. Clara followed. An old grey-haired man with a tic jerking his head stood at the door of Clara's bedroom.

"This is Mr. Rabinowitz," her mother said. "I've rented him a room…four dollars a week."

Clara's father said nothing. His face reddened. He gave the boarder a single nod, turned, and left the house.

After that, her parents stopped speaking to each other. Her father would toss the ten-dollar bill for the household expenses on the oilcloth of the kitchen table. Her mother would wait until he left the room before she picked it up.

The boarder moved out after two weeks, refusing the help of Clara's brothers with his two suitcases. He stumbled down the steps of the stoop, mumbling and shaking his head. Clara moved back into the small room.

Her father appeared to sink into himself. Sometimes Clara would see him staring at his wife's back as she worked in the kitchen. Once he stood in front of her and started to speak, but she turned and walked out of the room.

That summer, Clara's Uncle Harry and Aunt Lena, who lived on the next block, rented a house in the Catskill Mountains for two months to escape the sweltering streets of Brooklyn. They invited Clara's family to share their bungalow for two weeks.

On a damp July day, the family loaded the uncle's pickup truck. The boys and Clara sat on quilts on the floor of the truck while her mother squeezed into the cab with Aunt Lena and Uncle Harry. Clara's father stayed behind, reluctant to give up two weeks' wages. He stood on the stoop and waved at them as they pulled away. Clara held him in view until he went into the house.

When the family returned after two weeks, the boys barely said hello to their father and ran outside with their baseball gloves. Clara's father, his hair slicked down with a new hair-cut, his eyes smiling, stood in the living room before a luxuriant mural painted on the full expanse of the wall. Clara's mother came into the room, stood frozen before the wall for a few seconds, and let out a screech.

"What the hell is this?" she yelled. "What did you do? You're crazy...you son of a bitch!"

The smile in her father's eyes faded.

Clara stood transfixed before the landscape that graced the dingy parlor. It was a scene of a glistening lake surrounded by a lush green forest. In the center of the lake was a rowboat with the figure of a man, his rod a graceful arch, the fine fishing line sunk in the rippling water. Sunlight broke through the branches and cast a glow on the lake. As Clara stared at the mural, it seemed to slip out of focus, producing a kind of motion bringing it to life. She closed her eyes tight and tried to melt into this scene of serenity.

The next day, he painted over the mural with two coats of beige flat.

❧   ❧   ❧

Clara held the oil painting of the horse in her hands. She looked around her small living room for a place to hang it. A perfect spot was on the panel facing the window. She removed a framed work of petit point from the wall and put the gilt-framed painting in its place where the light from the window caught the thumbprint in the upper left corner.

HERE IN AMERICA

"Hannah, get me the magnifying glass."

Hannah put down the sock she was darning and found the eyeglass in a drawer. She leaned over her father's shoulder while he read the small print in the Jewish DAILY FORWARD spread out on the kitchen table.

"Look, Lena," he said to his wife. "The Rotterdam is arriving at Ellis Island tomorrow."

Hannah's mother wiped her hands on her apron. "That's Maryasha's boat, no?"

Hannah leaned closer and followed her father's finger on the steamship schedule. The S.S. Rotterdam would arrive on Saturday, December 1, 1908, at 10 A.M.

"We'll have to make a place for her," her mother said. She went to stand in the doorway to contemplate the front room parlor. "We'll move Hannah's bed out of David's room," she said. "The girls will sleep in the parlor."

Her father examined the calendar on the wall next to the icebox.

"Papa," Hannah said, "how come I never met your sister and her children when we lived in Russia?"

"Because Vlodstok is five hundred kilometers from Minsk. You think I'm a millionaire? The rail fare costs money."

That evening, Hannah almost knocked her brother over when he came home from work.

"Guess what, David? Maryasha's boat is landing tomorrow."

"So?" he said. He removed his coat and muffler. "I don't know what we need her for. We hardly have room for ourselves. What's for supper?"

"David, you be nice," his mother said. "She's your cousin. I don't want any trouble from you."

On Saturday, Hannah watched her father and brother prepare to leave for Ellis Island.

"Papa, why can't I go with you and David?"

"Hannah, don't you remember the tumult there? We could be there for days. Stay here. Help Mama make room for your cousin."

Hannah didn't argue. After three years, she still had nightmares about their torturous trip in steerage across the ocean. She could not forget the cramped quarters, the smell of urine, the moans of sick people, and the stench of vomit. She remembered their arrival at Ellis Island in New York Harbor, the crowds of tired, confused people standing in lines with their squirming children, their bundles at their feet.

When her father left the house with David, Hannah went to the front room parlor and looked out the window through the iron bars of the fire-escape to the street three floors below. She watched them board the trolley car that passed in front of their building.

It was a cold morning but Mrs. Chomskey, wrapped in her brown sweater with the holes in the elbows, leaned out on the window sill of her third floor apartment across the street. Mrs. Chomskey kept an eye on the trolley car to see who rode on the Sabbath and to keep track of the comings and goings of the neighbors. When she saw the father and son boarding the trolley, she looked across at Hannah's window. Hannah cupped her hands around her mouth. "They're going to Ellis Island to meet my cousin, Maryasha," she called. Mrs. Chomskey nodded her thanks.

On the street below, a few children skipped rope, some ran in circles like mice, and a group of *Hasidim*, in their long black coats and fur hats, walked from the *shul* on the next block. Yoineh, the rag collector, took up most of the sidewalk as he struggled down the street with two heavy bags that hung outward from his shoulders.

At five o'clock, Hannah settled at the window for one last watch. The street lamps lit up, one by one, as dusk settled on the street. At last, the trolley stopped at the corner. The door opened with a clang, and she saw her father step off the trolley, followed by David, and a skinny girl, wearing a heavy gray wool shawl over her head and shoulders just like all the "greeners" on their first day in America. Each of them carried a bundle wrapped in a pillow case tied with a rope.

"Mama, they're here," Hannah called into the flat. Her mother rushed to put up a pot of potatoes.

As soon as they came through the door, Maryasha was swamped by the family—Hannah's mother and her grandparents, who lived across the hall. Hannah's mother chirped like a bird and stroked Maryasha's cheeks. Bubbeh and Zaideh smiled and shook their old heads up and down. They all kissed and hugged Maryasha, ignoring her tears as she wiped her eyes and nose on her shawl.

When Maryasha was settled on the sofa in the front room, Hannah looked her over from head to foot. Two thick, blonde braids hung over her slender shoulders. Her skin was white as eggshells, her cheeks pink like roses. Fine pale freckles spread across her nose. Her eyes, sky blue, were red-rimmed from crying. She blushed a lot, and every once in a while she forced a weak smile, showing her small, even teeth. She could melt the heart of a Cossack, Hannah thought. David's gaze was on her as if caught by a magnet.

Hannah, seventeen, and two years older than Maryasha, assumed the responsibility of teaching her cousin how to get

along here in America. She led Maryasha around the flat showing her their yellow canary in its cage, the pull-chain on the toilet, and how the faucets worked. Maryasha tiptoed through the
rooms like a nervous chicken. Every ten minutes, she started to
cry.

That night in bed, Hannah asked her why she cried so much.

Maaryasha turned her face to the wall. "I miss my mother and
father and my little sister Bayleh, and Mishka, my donkey," she
said. "And that man in Ellis Island…I was so afraid…he said my
name is Mar-ee-a. He wrote it on a paper. Mar-ee-a is not my
name. My father told me to say that I am seventeen years old. I
am only fifteen. That man at Ellis Island…what if he finds out?
Hannah, is there a jail house here?"

"There's no jail house here. Nobody is going to find out. Go
to sleep, Maryasha."

The rattling of a trolley car passing below echoed in the room.
They lay without speaking for a minute. Then Maryasha whispered, "There are no trees here."

On Sunday, Maryasha sat in the kitchen to meet the neighbors who came in to look her over. David made lots of trips to
the icebox. Mrs. Rubin, from downstairs, brought her some blini
with apples. Maryasha was too embarrassed to say thank you.

At supper, Maryasha managed to swallow a tablespoon of
cabbage soup and a bite of bread. "Maryasha, you have to eat,"
her aunt said. "You'll need strength for your new life here in
America. You'll learn to speak English. As soon as you're settled, we'll help you find a job."

"Mama," Hannah said. "Mr. Klugel, from the factory, fired a
girl on Friday."

"Why?" her mother said. She started to clear the table. "What
happened?"

"It was Rosie. She picked up a scrap of material from the
floor and sewed herself a handkerchief. Mr. Klugel caught her
and fired her. Maybe Maryasha could take her job."

"Wait," Hannah's mother said. "I know Mr. Klugel's wife. She buys her chickens from Nate. I see her by the butcher every Friday. I know she lives on Pitkin Avenue in the two family house on the corner."

She removed her apron. "This is perfect. I'll go to his house and ask him to take Maryasha for the job. Hannah, get your coat. You'll go with me. Maryasha, you'll stay here. You should rest."

Hannah and her mother walked six blocks through the cold dark streets to Mr. Klugel's house, a grand brick house with a porch. Her mother rang the bell and Hannah stood behind her. Mrs. Klugel came to the door wearing an apron over her cotton print dress.

"Oh...hello, Lena. What a surprise. Didn't I see you Friday by the butcher?"

"Hello, Mrs. Klugel. You did see me by the butcher. But that was Friday. Today, I have some business. I came to see Mr. Klugel."

Mrs. Klugel invited them to sit in the neat kitchen. She passed an anxious look into the parlor where her husband was snoring in an easy chair. "I have some tea on the stove," she said. She placed three glasses of tea on the table, and peered again into the parlor. "Maybe he'll wake up soon." She stirred her tea with her spoon, creating a small clamor in the glass.

Mr. Klugel rose and came into the kitchen, scratching his ribs through his undershirt.

"Sam," Mrs. Klugel said. "Mrs. Schneider came to see you. She has something to say to you. It's business."

Klugel examined Hannah and her mother and gave no sign of recognition. He hooked his thumbs under his suspenders. "So, what's your business?" he said.

"Mr. Klugel, my daughter, Hannah, she works for you in the shop." She tilted her head toward her daughter.

"I know her," he said. "She's the second from the last machine."

Hannah blushed and looked at the floor.

"So, Hannah told me you lost one of your operators."

He shrugged. "So?"

"So, my niece…she lives with us…she's looking for a job."

"She knows how to operate a machine?"

"Sure. What do you think, she's a dummy?"

"How old is she?"

"She's eighteen. She's a smart girl. Don't worry."

"Where did she work before?"

"All over. She's a good worker."

Mr. Klugel sat down on a kitchen chair while his wife poured him a glass of tea.

"All right," he said. "We'll see. Send her with your daughter tomorrow."

On Monday, Hannah's mother packed two sandwiches of sardines and onions, and two apples in a paper bag, and gave them each six cents for carfare to and from the factory. Hannah told her cousin that here in America, the women do not wear shawls over their heads and shoulders even on such a cold morning. She gave Maryasha a sweater of hers to wear under her light coat. Maryasha's shoes were old with cracks in the leather. Hannah told her that as soon as she saved up one dollar, they would go to Delancey Street for new shoes.

They walked to the corner and waited for the trolley in front of Sasha's bakery. Maryasha stared at the trays of doughnuts and cakes in Sasha's window. So Hannah decided that they could each buy a cruller for three cents and walk the mile and a half home from work that evening.

They sat side by side in the trolley and ate their crullers. Maryasha peered around the car and twisted her body to look out the windows. After several stops, the door swung open, and an old black man in a threadbare gray coat and a filthy cap came into the car. Maryasha made a choking sound, and her eyes opened wide. She shifted close to Hannah as the man walked past them and took a seat. She grabbed Hannah's arm and held tight.

At the next stop, Maryasha jumped up, ran to the open door, and hopped out onto the street. Hannah followed just as the trolley door snapped shut. They stood on the corner, panting. Hannah looked at the trolley which was rumbling away. She had left their lunch on the seat.

"Maryasha, what happened?" she asked. "Why did you run out like that?"

"Hannah, did you see that man?" she gasped. "His face was black like a prune and his hands were black, too!"

Hannah rolled her eyes upward. "It's all right, Maryasha. Calm yourself." She explained to Maryasha about brown and black-skinned people who came here from Africa. Maryasha looked apprehensive.

They were only a few blocks from the Apex Waist Factory. Hannah told Maryasha some of the things she should know about the shop. "Everything will be fine," she said. "Just listen to the foreman and do everything he tells you."

As soon as Mr. Klugel saw Maryasha, a blush went up from his neck and across the top of his shiny bald head. When he learned that she could not work a sewing machine, he placed her where he could watch her from his table, and brought one of the women over to show her how to trim seams. Hannah couldn't see Maryasha from her place at the far end of the row of sixteen machines.

Around eleven o'clock, the long grimy windows in the shop turned dark gray. A few thin snowflakes fell on the glass and became muddy stains. Soon the flakes grew and came straight down in strong streaks.

When the bell rang for the thirty-minute lunch break, Hannah came to Maryasha's table. Mr. Klugel seemed to be satisfied with her work, although he said nothing. Some of the women offered them pieces of their sandwiches, but Maryasha was too shy to accept, so Hannah refused, also.

At four o'clock, Mr. Klugel came past Hannah's machine with Maryasha close behind him. Maryasha glanced at Hannah, and followed Mr. Klugel into the supply room. Hannah kept a nervous gaze on the closed door. After a few minutes, there was a loud noise, the supply room door flew open, and Maryasha rushed out. All the sewing machines stopped. A thick layer of black machine oil from an overturned can oozed out of the doorway onto the sewing room floor. Mr. Klugel had to lift his feet, one over the other, to step through the layer of oil. For a brief moment, Hannah wanted to laugh. Mr. Klugel's face and head were purple like an eggplant. He grabbed a finished waist from a basket and started to wipe the oil from his shoes. His eyes bulged. He turned to Hannah and screeched, "You're fired... both of you! Take that little witch and get out of here."

All the women stared. Maryasha was at the door in her coat. Tears ran down her cheeks.

"What about our pay?" Hannah said to Mr. Klugel.

"Your pay? Your pay?" he yelled. "That little 'greener' isn't getting any money. I should make her pay for that mess she made in there."

"But what about my pay?" Hannah mumbled.

"Payday is Friday. If you dare to come back Friday, you might get your wages for half a day."

They walked down the narrow stairway to the metal outer door. "Maryasha, what happened?"

Maryasha didn't need to explain. Hannah already knew.

"He asked me to get the machine oil down from the shelf, and all of a sudden he was standing close to me...and then he..." She clutched the buttons of her coat.

"Never mind," Hannah said.

When they stepped out onto the pavement, their shoes sank into three inches of snow. The streets were empty, since the factories had not let out yet. After walking a few blocks, their heads and shoulders were covered with snow. They linked arms, trying to hold one another up on the icy sidewalk. The wind stabbed through their wet coats and stung their cheeks. A trolley rattled on its tracks as it passed.

"I wish I had my shawl," Maryasha said, and she started to cry.

"Maryasha, stop pee-ing with your eyes," Hannah yelled. "You're always pee-ing with your eyes!"

The street lamps came on one by one, and the snowflakes danced like gold dust under the lights. Their shoes were soaked through.

"I'm hungry," Maryasha wailed. "And I'm cold. I wish I were back home in Vlodstok."

"So do I," Hannah hollered. "You made me lose my job."

Hannah grabbed Maryasha's sleeve and tried to pull her along, but Maryasha slipped on the ice and they both went down, rolling in the snow.

"We'll never be able to go home," Maryasha cried. "We'll be buried in the snow. Nobody will ever find us." She looked up at the sky as if searching for a miracle.

Suddenly a change swept over her face. She stared at the street sign and struggled to her feet.

"What is that word?" she asked. "What does it say?"

Hannah looked at the street sign. "It says Chester Street."

"I know that street," she said. "When my mother wrote letters to her friend in America, I used to write that street on the envelope...One ninety-two Chester Street."

"What are you talking about? Let's go." Hannah grabbed her sleeve again and tried to pull her across the street.

"No, listen to me. My mother's friend lives on this street. Rachel Berkowitz. She came over two years ago. I used to help my mother write to her. She lives on this street."

"Rachel Berkowitz? Rachel the Redhead is your mother's friend?"

Maryasha stared.

"Everybody knows Rachel the Redhead," Hannah said. "We are not allowed to say her name in our house."

Maryasha said, "I don't understand."

Hannah lowered her voice, although there was nobody to hear them.

"Everybody in our neighborhood knows that she does business when her husband goes to work every day."

"Business?"

"Business…monkey business."

"I don't understand."

"Look," Hannah said. "Rachel the Redhead entertains men in her house." She moved closer. "In the bathtub, so her husband won't find any signs of the men in their bed."

The dawn of understanding settled on Maryasha's face.

They stood for a minute in silence, their frozen feet buried up to their ankles, while the snowflakes hopped and teased their faces in an icy dance.

Maryasha turned away and started to walk down Chester Street. She shaded her eyes with her hands as she looked up at the numbers over the doors of the three-story brick houses. Hannah followed, tugging at her sleeve, but Maryasha pulled her arm away. They argued as they walked. Hannah's words were lost on her cousin as she pushed ahead. After a block and a half, Maryasha stopped.

"One ninety-two. That's the number. One ninety-two Chester Street. Come on. We could go in there to warm up."

"I won't have anything to do with that woman," Hannah said.

Maryasha's tears started to flow again. "We'll never get home," she cried. "We'll die on the street. I just want to warm up a little," she begged.

"Well, you can go in. I won't go into that house."

But she followed Maryasha past the heavy wooden door. Once inside, Maryasha stopped, not knowing which way to turn in the dark hallway. With a sigh, Hannah moved to a small light over the tarnished brass mail boxes on the wall. Maryasha followed and stood next to her cousin. Her breath bounced off the wall like an echo, as Hannah read the names.

"Berkowitz, 2B" she said. "I'll take you to her flat, but I will not go in. I'll wait in the hall."

They walked up to the second floor leaving puddles on the creaking wooden stairs. A small bare bulb in the ceiling lit the landing. At Apartment 2B, Hannah rang the bell and stepped away against the wall.

When the door opened, the smell of food and a rush of warmth passed into the hall from the kitchen. Rachel stood in the doorway. "Maryasha...my little Maryasha. Your mother wrote that you were coming, but I didn't know you were here already." She swung her head out into the hall and smiled at Hannah. She pulled both girls into the bright, warm kitchen.

Rachel was a short buxom woman with a pretty face and a mop of red curls. There was a happy twinkle in her brown eyes, and Rachel seemed gentle and warm, just like Hannah's own mother, all of which offended Hannah. She did not want to be taken in by such a woman. When Rachel invited them to remove their coats, she made no move. Maryasha shot a pleading look at her, so out of kindness to her cousin, she removed her coat, and Maryasha did the same.

Hannah asked to use the toilet. Behind the door, she could not resist a fast look into the bathtub. Going out of the bathroom, she met Maryasha coming in. "Ask to borrow six cents for the trolley," she whispered.

Rachel insisted that they sit at the kitchen table that was covered by blue and yellow flowered oil cloth. She moved back and forth from the stove to the icebox to the sink, turning her head to listen as Maryasha told her about the job at the waist factory. Maryasha did not mention that they had been fired.

"This morning we bought crullers with our carfare…and now look how it's snowing…would you be so kind…we need six cents for the trolley. I promise we'll pay it back."

Rachel immediately took some change out of a jar and handed it to Maryasha.

"Jake will be home any minute," Rachel said. "You'll have something to eat with us."

Maryasha gave an apprehensive glance at her cousin. "No, thank you," she said. "We have to go home, soon." Hannah's heart sank. The smell of food made her head spin.

When Rachel's husband came home, Hannah observed him with interest. She had heard that he was a Socialist and a freethinker and went to those rowdy union meetings that were reported in the newspaper. When he entered, his eyeglasses clouded over from the heat in the kitchen and gave him a sinister look. But as he removed his coat, his eyeglasses cleared. His soft gray eyes appeared and sent a smiling, questioning look at the girls.

"Jake, see who's here," Rachel said. "You remember little Maryasha from Vlodstok. She just came over on the Rotterdam. She's staying with her aunt and uncle from Amboy Street. This is her cousin, Hannah."

"Maryasha, you've grown so tall," he said. "A regular beauty. Welcome to America."

Rachel set the table while they talked.

"Come on," she said. "You'll have something to eat with us… at least a glass of tea?"

Hannah poked Maryasha with her elbow hoping she would accept, but Maryasha looked at the floor. "No, no, we're not hungry. We'll be leaving in a few minutes."

Rachel carried a bowl of hot mashed potatoes to the table with a loaf of dark brown bread, a slab of butter, and a plate of sliced herring with onions in sour cream. Jake helped himself to several slices of herring. Hannah's gaze followed the strands of onions from the plate to his lips. A pot of barley soup simmered on the stove.

"Why won't you eat something girls? You need some meat on your bones." She squeezed Maryasha's arm. "How do you expect to catch a bridegroom?"

Maryasha blushed and shook her head. Hannah's eyes filled with tears of frustration. She almost choked on her saliva. Why is Maryasha such a goose? Surely it couldn't hurt to have just one glass of tea? Maybe a piece of bread and butter?

"I think it stopped snowing," Maryasha said. "We have to go now." The girls put on their soggy coats. "I'll come to see you soon."

They walked down the creaking stairs. Maryasha grasped Hannah's sleeve, but Hannah jerked her arm away. They said not a word through the quiet dark streets to the corner trolley stop, nor did they talk all the way home in the rattling car.

Hannah ate like a wolf at supper. Maryasha nibbled on a heel of bread. Hannah explained to the family about Mr. Klugel and how they lost their jobs, but she did not mention Rachel the Redhead.

In their bed that night, Hannah looked through the window at the sky, calm and smooth as glass. She thought she saw a few stars.

Their shoulders touched. Hannah turned to her cousin. "The storm has passed," she said. It will be fine here in America. You'll see. It will be fine." She pulled the blanket up under her chin. "Goodnight, Maryasha."

"Goodnight," Maryasha said.

VOODOO MAN

George climbed the stairs and stood outside the bathroom door. He listened for the hum of his son's electric razor to stop. When Steve came out, George said, "Your wife is trying to kill me."

Steve swept past him. "Dad, I'm running late. I have to get going."

"But I thought you should know. Yesterday she put poison in my soup."

George followed Steve to his bedroom and leaned into the doorway while his son dressed.

"Dad, you've got to get ahold of yourself. Marcia is doing the best she can for you. Now, come downstairs and have your breakfast, and behave yourself."

In the kitchen, Marcia poured coffee, and the three of them ate cold cereal. The ticking of the Black Forest clock on the wall covered their silence. At eight o'clock, the doors of the clock snapped open, and a jaunty little bird popped out. "Coo-coo," it screeched. "Coo-coo." Steve took a last swallow of coffee and stood up. "See you later," he said. He kissed Marcia on the cheek, picked up his briefcase at the door, and left for work.

Marcia started to clear the table. George rose and followed her to the sink where he stationed himself close behind her.

"I know you're trying to kill me," he said.

"Oh, for heaven's sake, George!"

"You've been putting poison in my food."

"Nobody's putting anything into your food."

"You can't fool me. I can taste it. I told Steve about it…how you put poison in my soup yesterday."

"For God's sake, George. Don't bother Steve with such non-sense. He doesn't need this."

"Nonsense? It's not nonsense. You think I can't taste that stuff you put in my food?"

"Look, can we drop this? You're always causing trouble. We can be friends or enemies…it's up to you."

"How can we be friends when you're trying to poison me?"

"You're a crazy old man. You're going to have to trust me. We can't live together otherwise."

"Oh, so that's it. Now you're threatening me. Well, Steve won't have it. He won't send me back to Vista Care with all those old loonies."

Marcia turned from the sink to face him. "Well, maybe you belong with those old loonies." She dried her hands on a towel. "I've got to get to work. Let me pass."

George went out the back door to the yard and sat in a webbed garden chair. The event of the night before returned to cause a sick rumble in his chest. The Voodoo man had come again to stand beside his bed speaking his gibberish. George had rolled out of bed and run across the room knocking a table lamp to the floor. That had brought Steve and Marcia rushing down to his room in their nightclothes.

Steve swung the door open. "Dad, are you all right? What happened?"

"Oh, nothing…nothing."

Marcia looked around the room. "What's all the commotion about? I'll bet you were having one of those dreams again."

"No, no…I wasn't having a dream. I was trying to swat a mosquito."

"Steve, what are we going to do about this?" Marcia said. "We can't put up with these shenanigans every night."

"Calm down, Marcia." Steve put the lamp upright. "We'll talk about this in the morning." He turned to his father. "Go back to sleep."

George rose from the garden chair and walked around the edge of the yard passing under a weeping willow. He pulled a few weeds from a flower bed, removed a pair of his socks that hung next to Marcia's lace tablecloth on the clothes line in the center of the yard, and went back into the house.

Once in his room, he looked into the mirror over his dresser and smoothed his gray wisps of hair. He searched in his reflection for the dark brown incisive eyes, diminished now by a rheumy film. Sometimes when he gazed into a mirror, memories of lost opportunities and bygone blunders emerged to pique him. In a strange way, these images were not unwelcome. Like pain from a splinter, they made him feel alive. They endowed him with a history—a lifeline against the vacuum of his future.

At dinner, the asparagus tasted suspicious. He moved the stalks to the edge of his plate.

The next morning, he stood at the bottom of the stairway wondering if he should go up and tell Steve about the asparagus, but Steve came down the stairs and said, "Listen, Dad, Marcia's having her Saturday bridge club here for lunch today. So don't give her a hard time. Can you promise me that?"

When Steve rose from the breakfast table to leave for work, Marcia followed him to the door. George heard them talking.

"Did you speak to him?" she said.

"I spoke to him. He won't give you any trouble."

Marcia returned to her seat at the table. "George, are you okay this morning?"

"Why shouldn't I be?" He looked into his coffee cup.

"I just meant…you haven't been sleeping well."

"I'm sleeping fine, just fine."

"Are you going out for your newspaper?"

"Maybe."

"Would you pick up a dozen dinner rolls for me at the Bread Basket?"

"All right."

"Could you go now? I need the rolls for the luncheon. The women are coming at twelve o'clock."

George put on his sweater and checked his back pocket for his wallet. He peered into the dining room where the air-conditioner was already blowing cool air. He observed the gleaming wood table, the china closet with its shining figurines and dinnerware. The living room, also, looked forbidding—the TV cabinet closed, newspapers and magazines hidden, sofa pillows puffed. The message was clear. Off limits.

He went out and started down the walk, yielding to the stippled sunshine that pushed through the maple trees edging the street. He crossed at the corner, bought his paper at the newsstand, and went to the bakery next door where he bought the rolls and three blueberry muffins.

Outside the store, the sounds of children playing drew him toward the school playground across the street. As soon as he sat down on a bench, a small boy approached. The boy was about six years old, with the obvious features of Downs Syndrome, his blue eyes narrowed by puffed lids and his tongue laying like a warm loaf on his lower lip. The child raised his arms, and George lifted him to the space beside him on the bench. They looked at each other.

"She's trying to kill me," George said. "She puts poison in my food."

The boy smiled.

"She's trying to get rid of me. She's mad because I wouldn't stay in the nursing home they sent me to after my Dora died." He took a muffin out of the bag, removed the pleated paper, and handed it to the boy.

Blueberry muffins, small and pasty, had been served that first day at Vista Care. An image of the bedroom rose, stern and alien, stiff green drapes at the window, and hard, plastic furniture. And there was the smell that hung in every corner. He could not escape the odor even that first night when he buried his face into the pillow.

The next day, a tiny, scrawny black man came into his room. The man had a yellowish-white eyeball which stood stationery in its socket while the other eye roamed around. George ran out of the room, but the man followed. All that day, the man stayed with him, tugging at his sleeve and speaking gibberish.

George recalled his frantic phone calls to Steve at work. "I can't stay here," he whimpered. "That little man is trying to do something to me. He's a Voodoo man." Steve phoned the house administrator who assured him that the little man was suffering from Alzheimers and was harmless. But George knew better.

When Steve and Marcia brought George home to live with them, Marcia had to give up her sewing room and store her Singer and patterns and fabrics in the garage. At dinner, on George's first night in their home, the conversation was stiff and subdued. Every clink of a fork reverberated in the room.

When the Voodoo man started to appear at their home and stand by George's bed at night, Steve told George he was dreaming. It was true that his dreams baffled him—the nights colliding with the days, merging like a shuffling deck of cards, producing little terrors and confusions with no separation between dreams and reality.

George looked at the boy beside him. "There was a medicine man in that place," he said. "At night he came into my room and stood near my bed saying magic things. He was practicing Voodoo on me."

The boy swallowed the last morsel of his muffin. He looked up and said, "More." But George stood and said, "I gotta go now, little fella."

On Maple Street, George started to count the houses from the corner. Ever since a tree had been removed, the street looked different, and once he had tried to enter a neighbor's house.

As soon as he opened the door, Marcia called from the top of the stairs, "George, where have you been? It's almost eleven o'clock. Did you stop at the bakery?"

"Yes," George said.

"There's a sandwich in the fridge for your lunch. Can you take it into your room? Leave the rolls on the counter."

Rolls? He didn't have them. In his mind's eye, he saw the white bakery bag on the park bench.

"George, I'm running late. Would you bring the lace table-cloth in from the yard?"

George opened the refrigerator to get his sandwich. On the middle shelf a stately orange and green Jello mold sat on a silver tray. He picked up a spoon, dug into the dessert and swallowed a huge mouthful. He took the sandwich to his bedroom at the back of the house and then went out to the yard.

What had Marcia said about the table cloth? He shuffled across the lawn where a chaise invited him from the shade of the willow. He sat down, put his head back on the stiff plastic webs, and closed his eyes. He entered at once into a dream state. He felt as if his body were suspended, his knuckles taut around something cold and metallic. The Voodoo man appeared. This time George thought he could make out some words in the stream of gibberish. "Let go," he heard. A few more words emerged in the babble…"Let go. It's too hard." A torrent of jabbering, and then the words, crystal clear now, "Let go, George. Let go. Come with me."

His eyes popped open. He heard the snap of the Black Forest clock from the kitchen. "Coo-coo, Coo-coo," wafted across the yard.

He saw Marcia upstairs at the mirror near the open bathroom window applying her makeup. George rose from the chaise and started to circle the line where the lace tablecloth stirred in the breeze. Marcia looked out of the window, her head tilted, her gaze fixed on him. He fumbled with his zipper. Then, he faced the clothes line and let loose a watery, golden arc projecting up and over onto the tablecloth. He thought he heard Marcia's voice.

An overwhelming fatigue washed over him. George stumbled into the house and lay on his bed to wait for the Voodoo man.

THE HOLIDAYS

When Uncle Itchy got married, nobody was invited to the wedding. He came home one day from a business trip to Detroit with a new 1935 car and a new wife. He didn't bring his wife around to introduce her, and there was a rumor in the neighborhood that she wasn't Jewish. It was December, and there was another rumor—that he had a Christmas tree in his house.

The day came when he couldn't avoid us any more. It was the Chanukah party at our house. Every year Mama makes a hundred potato *latkes* and thick apple sauce for the party. All our relatives come—uncles, aunts, and cousins—which is a good thing, because the uncles and aunts give the children Chanukah *gelt*. Most of my uncles give me a quarter and they give my two older brothers fifty cents each. Uncle Itchy gives me only a dime, and he gives my brothers a quarter each.

This year, Uncle Itchy did a strange thing. He gave us presents wrapped in fancy paper with ribbons instead of Chanukah *gelt*. I got a book, "The Princess and the Goblins," and my brothers got a pair of boxing gloves—one pair for the two of them. Uncle Itchy said he thought that would be all right since Jake was a lefty and Philly was a righty, so they could each use one glove.

The fact that we got presents instead of Chanukah *gelt* made us more suspicious about Itchy's wife whose name was Margaret. She was very pretty with a turned up nose and blue eyes, and she talked kind of funny, saying her "R's" very sharp, like they do in the movies. Nobody asked Uncle Itchy if his wife was a *shikseh*, and everyone was very polite, except for Mr. Rabinowitz, our boarder, who refused to come out of his room.

When the *latkes* were served, Margaret leaned across the table toward Uncle Itchy and said, "Irwin (she always called Uncle Itchy "Irwin"), is there any ketchup for these home fries?" That's when we knew the truth.

Everything is different around the holidays. Like the time just before Passover when we had a live carp in our bathtub that Mama had ordered special from Mr. Rivkin's fish store. I heard Mama tell Mrs. Krantz from next door that the fish had cost three dollars.

"Fresh!" she told Mrs. Krantz. "The fish has to be fresh." Which was why the carp was in the bathtub. I watched him from my place on the toilet seat. He was two feet long and there wasn't much room for him to swim. His eyes accused me. Someone in the house would have to kill the big fish. I knew my brothers' baseball bat reckoned in the situation. I also knew that neither my brother Jake or my brother Philly could do the job. They were mean, but not enough to kill the fish. Papa couldn't either. No, it would have to be Mama. After all, Mama had a responsibility—the gefilte fish for the holidays. Mama made enough for the family to eat every day of Passover plus enough for some relatives and special neighbors.

The doorknob of the bathroom jiggled. I looked down at the carp and whispered, "Good-bye," because I didn't know if I would ever see the fish again in its life. When I came out, I bumped into Mr. Rabinowitz.

"Aye, Basha, you were in there so long I thought you fell into the bowl." I tried to slip by him, but he grabbed my cheek and delivered a painful, wiggling pinch. I rubbed my face and went to watch Mama prepare the horseradish.

"Tell him not to pinch me, Mama."

"Never mind, Basha. It's because he loves you."

"Why does he always have to be the boss?"

Mr. Rabinowitz is not much taller than I am, and I am only nine, but somehow around the holidays, he seems to be taller. That's because he is so religious. He walks around the house with his bible tucked under his arm, muttering into his bushy gray beard and shaking his head which seems too big for such a little man. "*Hazerim*—Pigs!" he yells if anyone slips up on the rules, and his thick black eyebrows jump up and down like two furry animals.

When Uncle Itchy and his wife were invited to our Passover seder, Margaret's mother and sister were visiting from Detroit, so Mama had to invite them too. The sister was ten years old and wore a yellow organdy Easter dress. Margaret's mother brought a large bowl of clam dip and a bag of potato chips. Papa had to take Mr. Rabinowitz out of the room and gave him a cold compress. Mama, by accident, dumped the clam dip into the toilet bowl. Later, the little sister told me that Mama's gefilte fish tasted like pissy cat food.

Because of Mr. Rabinowitz the family is careful not to break any of the rules for the holidays. For one thing, Papa, who never goes to *shul* during the year, puts on his blue suit at Rosh Hashanah and goes to services where he meets Uncle Aaron and some friends. Jake and Philly have to go, too.

For a week before Rosh Hashanah, the family hops around like jumping beans. Mama scrubs and polishes and dusts and brings out the good dishes and the stiff white tablecloths. She washes the curtains in the parlor, and my brothers have to clean the windows.

It happened that this year there was a mouse living in our kitchen and it ran across the room at night whenever someone turned the light on. Mama was embarrassed to have a mouse in the flat during Rosh Hashanah. So she gave my brothers twenty cents to buy a trap, and she put them in charge of getting rid of the mouse. But my brothers spent the twenty cents for cigarettes at Mr. Kossokoff's candy store, so they had to come up with a different idea.

Three nights before Rosh Hashanah they put their plan in motion. After everyone was asleep, they got out of bed and took their places in the dark kitchen. Jake stood very still near the kitchen light switch, and Philly lay on the floor with his B-B gun ready. They were very still for fifteen minutes and at a signal from Philly, Jake turned the light on. The mouse ran across the kitchen linoleum and Philly let loose two quick shots. The mouse disappeared under the ice-box, but one of the B-B's found its mark in the tin drip pan underneath.

Mama, when she heard the noise, came running out of the bedroom and gave a loud scream when she found her feet and the hem of her nightgown in a puddle of water. Mr. Rabinowitz, whose small bedroom was off the kitchen, came out in his long underwear and yelled some foreign words which none of us had ever heard before.

As usual the family went to Millman's Department Store for new outfits for Rosh Hashona—except for my brother Jake who had to wear Philly's suit from last year. This year I got a pair of "Mary Jane's" like Peggy Clancy wears to Church.

On Yom Kippur Mama says I don't have to fast because I am under thirteen, but I want to anyway, except sometimes for a jawbreaker which I keep in my cheek all day. Even Brownie, our dog, has to fast. Mama takes away his dish and he follows her around the house, drooling. Mr. Rabinowitz watches the family like a hawk. It's a good thing he never found out what happened last year on Yom Kippur:

As usual the *shul* was most crowded during the part of the service when the Ark is opened. Last year I was anxious to be there so that I could ask God to erase my sins because of the time Georgy, the landlady's son, took me down to the cellar and made me look while he pulled his pants down.

So around the middle of the service, I went with Mama to the *shul*. Mama found a seat in the women's side and opened the prayer book. I stood at the back and looked through the rows of men rocking and praying to see if I could find Papa. It was so hot in the *shul*, it smelled like someone forgot to take out the garbage. Papa stood next to Uncle Aaron. He held the prayer book with one hand and wiped his brow with a damp handkerchief. After a few minutes, I went outside to join my friends who were playing "potsy" on the sidewalk.

When Papa and Uncle Aaron came out, I was not surprised because I knew the men often came out for five or ten minutes and stood in their prayer shawls just outside the door to get some air. But instead of standing near the door with the other men, Papa and Uncle Aaron edged back from the group and started down the street in the direction of our house. A few minutes later, Jake and Philly came out and wandered through the group of men who were standing around. I saw them whispering, and then they started to walk back toward our house. I followed them.

"Where are you going?" I called.

"Nowhere...stay there!" Philly yelled.

They were walking fast and I ran after them.

"Stop following us, you fat brat," Jake hollered.

The boys were almost running now as they came near the house. At the stoop, they stopped and looked around. I stopped, too, several paces away and watched them. They seemed to be discussing something serious as they went up the steps. I started after them. From the top of the stoop Jake shook his fist at me. After a few minutes I followed them into the hallway and could hear my brothers walking up the creaking wooden stairs. When I met up with them on the landing just below the third floor, Philly put his forefinger up to his lips. They walked up the last flight to our flat and tried the doorknob. It was locked. They jiggled the knob, and we heard some sounds from behind the door. Philly put his key into the lock and released the latch, but the door wouldn't budge.

"Who's there?" Papa's voice called from behind the door.

"It's me, Philly."

"What do you want? Why aren't you in *shul*? The services are almost over. The Rabbi will soon be blowing the *shofar*."

"Why aren't you in *shul* Papa? Don't you want to hear the *shofar*?"

"I came home because I have a headache."

"Is Uncle Aaron there?"

"He came with me to make sure I'm all right. Go back to *shul* you little *mamzer*. You're going to get it from me. Get away from the door."

"Let me in. I have to go to the bathroom."

We heard whispering, the sound of something heavy being moved away from the door, some more scuffling noises, and the sound of the ice-box slamming shut. When Papa opened the door, a whiff of onions floated into the hall. Papa grabbed Philly by the collar of his shirt and pulled him into the kitchen. Jake and I followed. There were some dishes in the sink. The table was covered with bread crumbs, and Uncle Aaron was trying to hide a pumpernickel behind his back. Papa gave Philly several hard slaps across his shoulder.

We raced down the steps in the hallway, jumped down the stoop, and ran several blocks to the *shul*. There was still time to hear the Rabbi blow the *shofar*.

THE BARN

My heart ached for Aunt Belle who stood dry-eyed in the cold December air. Only nine people were present at the burial site to see Uncle Ivan to his rest.

When the ceremony began with the droning of the rabbi's words, my brother Jack moved to the rear of the little group and leaned against a tree like a happenstance onlooker. Stan, the older of my two brothers, turned and glared at him, but Jack stood his ground. There we were, a pitiful handful of the remaining Povich family, our hearts brimming with mutual affection and sadness. So, that was it. The end of Uncle Ivan, a man who had garnered so much love in his lifetime.

In the black limousine that was part of the burial package, Aunt Belle sat silent on the plush seat, staring straight ahead, flanked on each side by her children, Mike and Ellen. My two brothers and I sat in the seat facing them. Ellen dabbed at her eyes with a soggy tissue, but Aunt Belle's face was a cold façade for what must have been churning inside her. She had not wept in the chapel, nor at the grave, not even as the casket was lowered into the ground.

At her house in Liberty, one hundred miles north of New York City, we moved about the rooms making small talk, while Aunt Belle rested in her bedroom. When the few friends who had stood with us at the burial left, we settled in the large country kitchen and picked at a chicken casserole brought over by a neighbor. Aunt Belle joined us at the table, but she refused the food.

Later, my cousin Ellen brought out a photo album that she set on the kitchen table. "Look at this," she said. "I haven't seen these pictures in years."

Aunt Belle rose to move to the living room where she sat in a rocker, her heft filling the wooden frame of the chair.

Ellen opened the album. I sat next to her, and my brothers stood behind her looking over her shoulder. The first page had a photo of Aunt Belle and Uncle Ivan taken in a studio. Aunt Belle, in a slender brocade dress stood beside Uncle Ivan who was seated on a wrought iron chair. He wore a formal dark suit with a white collar pushing his head erect. His hair was slicked back tamping his thick dark curls. Aunt Belle's small pale hand rested on his shoulder.

"This was their engagement photo taken in Russia before they came to the States with your parents," Ellen said.

On the next page was a small glossy snapshot showing the two couples sitting on a stoop in front of a six-family house. Aunt Belle, in a white summer dress, and Uncle Ivan, in shirt-sleeves, sat on the top step. My mother, in a print blouse and skirt, and my father, wearing a straw hat, sat on a lower step. All four of them gazed into the camera with self-conscious box-camera smiles.

Stan said, "That must have been taken when we all lived on Dumont Avenue in Brooklyn. There's the number on the build-ing—one twenty-seven."

The rest of the photos brought smiles from the five of us, now in our thirties and forties, who dominated the remainder of the album. Most of the snapshots had been taken during the sum-mers on the Povich Brothers Farm in Liberty, about eight miles out of the town.

There was a photo of Ellen and me when she was nine, and I was six, standing barefoot before an iron hand pump in front of the big house. We wore identical dresses covering our knees, heads tilted toward one another, our dark curls blending. Other snapshots showed my cousin, Mike, and my brothers, Jack and Stan, doing acrobatics on the lawn.

The name "Povich Brothers Farm" was pretentious, for, while it had been a real farm long before my father and his brother bought the property, there were no chickens or cows on the grounds when we were growing up. No crops grew on the uneven turf. A vacant, sun-baked barn stood on a sunken foundation a hundred feet from the big house in a field of tangled weeds and goldenrod. The barn was the only remnant of the property's former function.

My father and uncle had converted the big house, as we called it, to a summer rooming house, a business venture to support the brothers and their young wives when they first came as immigrants to New York City. The big house had ten bedrooms, each large enough to accommodate a family. There was a commercial sized kitchen, and a large dining room with ten tables for the families. After a few years, four bungalows were added with eight more bedrooms, and "the farm" became a profitable business.

The roomers came for the entire summer, sharing the two bathrooms in the big house. In the kitchen were three stoves. The women followed a schedule for their use. Frequent arguments broke out. Nevertheless, the same roomers came back summer after summer—satisfied with the arrangements—glad to be away from the steamy pavements of Brooklyn or the Bronx.

My father, a quiet, troubled man, remained in our city apartment during July and August to maintain the house painting business which he shared with Uncle Ivan. He would come up weekends. Uncle Ivan stayed on the farm during the summers to minister to the frequent breakdowns in the creaking old house. Beds collapsed, the cesspool backed up, ice-boxes leaked, the water pump failed, rats and mice needed rooting from closets, and the roof was in constant disrepair. Uncle Ivan handled these burdens with good-natured aplomb. He was the surrogate father for my brothers and me during the summers.

When Ellen closed the photo album, Aunt Belle came back into the kitchen and sat with us. There was no sign she had given way to her grief. In her face was little evidence of the beauty she had once been. I reflected on her gentle, fragile nature which seemed now to have been replaced by an enigmatic strength.

I looked around the table. "Do you remember when Uncle Ivan came to my rescue with the oatmeal?"

"Of course," Ellen said. "But tell the story again. I don't think my Mom's ever heard it."

"I haven't," my aunt said.

"Well, Aunt Belle, I'll never forget that day. Do you remember my mother's fixation about my morning oatmeal?"

Aunt Belle nodded, smiling.

"Boy, I sure remember it," Stan said. "Jack and I both went through it with her."

"I must have been about nine then," I said. "I was sitting in the dining room with my back to the window with that bowl of cold, gray oatmeal in front of me. My friends were outside choosing up sides for a baseball game. Mama came to the door to threaten me. 'Don't you leave this room until that oatmeal is finished.' Just then, Uncle Ivan came in with a ladder to change a light bulb." I turned to Ellen. "Do you remember those canvas overalls your Dad used to wear with all the pockets, and that painter's cap with the visor turned to the back?"

"I can just see him," Ellen said.

"Well, he placed the ladder under the light bulb and said to me, 'What are you doing here, Anitchka? Your friends are waiting for you outside.' Mama glared at him and went back to the kitchen. He changed the bulb and left.

"I was staring at the oatmeal when I heard a scratching sound behind me. There was Uncle Ivan, perched on the ladder outside the window. He took a tool from his pocket and made an L-shaped slice in the screen."

Aunt Belle gasped. "You mean he cut open the screen?"

"Yeah, that's what he did. He put his arm right through over my shoulder and picked up my spoon. He took three spoons-ful of the cereal and swallowed them. Then, he took two more which emptied the bowl."

Mike said, "What if your mother had come in right then?"

"Believe me, my heart was rattling like a rock in a hollow tree. I heard Uncle Ivan fold the ladder. He was whistling as he walked away. After a minute, I yelled, 'Mama!'

"She came to the doorway and I pushed the bowl to the center of the table. She gave me a little smirk. I got up and ran out to the ball game."

Stan laughed. "God, Mom was a battle-axe."

"Your mother was a very strong and capable woman," Aunt Belle said. "She managed to keep the place running smoothly. I certainly wasn't much help."

"Of course, you were, Aunt Belle," I said. "You did all the paper work, and you were always there to keep peace among the roomers." I leaned over and kissed her cheek. "You had that sweet way about you. Even Uncle Ivan, with all his kidding around, couldn't break up a brawl between the women."

"He was such a lovable clown," Stan said. "Remember how he was always pulling surprises out of his pockets for the kids? And how about his old accordion? He'd sit on the ground under the lilac tree near the big house, playing the accordion with that far-away look in his eyes. The kids would crowd around, and he'd let them take turns playing chords on the old yellow keys."

I hoped Jack would add something, but he stood and stretched. "We should get an early start tomorrow if we want to go up to see the farm." We rose, kissed Aunt Belle, and went to bed. Jack and Stan took one room. Mike made up the sofa for himself. Ellen and I shared a double bed in another room.

Ellen's presence next to me in bed triggered a childhood wrinkle. Once, when I was about ten, I said to Ellen, "I wish I was your sister instead of your cousin." She had been putting my hair up in pincurls as we stood in front of the dresser mirror. She laughed. "We are just like sisters, silly," she said. "Look, we have the same wild and woolly hair and the same hazel eyes."

"Let's pretend we are sisters, okay?" I said.

"Okay."

That memory filled my eyes with tears. I looked across the pillow at my cousin. She was asleep, breathing in a steady rhythm.

It was a raw, sunless morning when we gathered for breakfast the next day. It had snowed during the night, and three inches of powder settled on the town. The plows had already passed through our street and created barricades around our cars. The plan was for all of us to go up together to see the farm, now owned by a large family as a vacation retreat. But by the time we shoveled our cars free, Stan said it was too late and he would start back to the city right away. Ellen and Mike decided to stay at the house with their mother.

My brother, Jack, had driven me up to Liberty, and we planned to start back to New York City after visiting the farm. We said our good-byes and set off on NY Route 17.

I scanned the sides of the road and talked non-stop, pointing out familiar landmarks—Kelly's Kustard, Buster's Auto Repair, Sally's Bar & Grill. We slowed down as we neared the dirt road that intersected the paved highway. Dewey Carr's Dairy still displayed its huge sign close to the shoulder at the narrow dirt road that led to the farm. The snow had almost obliterated the familiar road, but we turned in, tamping the fresh snow under the wheels, riding for about a mile, flanked on each side by snow-mottled Pines. My eyes swept the snow bank as we neared a clearing in the woods where a huge electrical power structure was enclosed in a chain link fence. The words DANGER! HIGH VOLTAGE! on a red and yellow plate high on the fence sent a reminiscent spark through me.

"Look, Jack, there's the power station," I said. "Remember how scared we used to be when we passed this monster on foot?"

Jack turned, then jammed his foot on the brake. The car skidded off the bank.

"Damn!" he said. A group of wild turkeys had come out of the woods and were passing in front of us. We watched as they huddled together and walked across the road, their red wattles flashing against the snow.

"Damn it, Annie," Jack said. "Can't you shut up until we get there? It's no picnic driving on this icy road."

"God, you've been a grizzly bear for two days," I said. "What's the matter with you?"

"What do you mean?"

"You were sulking in the car all the way up from the city. At the funeral you walked away from the grave during the ceremony. And another thing, you didn't even have one kind word to say about Uncle Ivan at the house."

"So?"

"The whole time we were talking you had that pinched pug-face that you get when you're angry."

"I can't believe what a Pollyanna you are," he mumbled.

"What's that supposed to mean? What's going on?"

"Nothing's going on, Annie. Just forget it."

"I can't forget it. Something's bugging you, and it's very obvious."

But I did forget it. My spirits rose as we approached the turn-off to the farm. The big house stood before us. The iron hand pump in front of it was still there, painted yellow. There was no road visible under the snow. We knew the house was vacant in the winter months, so Jack rode up as close as possible. The lilac bush was still there, snow capping its limbs, the subliminal scent of long-gone blossoms almost insinuating itself in the icy air. Green shutters had been put on the windows, and a new rail had been built enclosing the front porch. The four bungalows were painted white and looked elegant.

"Let's go see the orchard," I said. We walked past the house and stood on the crest of a downward slope leading to a spread of snow-topped apple trees. They stood with their spindly branches spread outward and downward like a crowd of bickering crones. "Remember the green apple fights we used to have? How carefree we were," I said.

Jack turned, so I followed him back to the big house. "Something's missing," I said looking around.

"It's the old barn," Jack said. "It's gone."

We walked across the lawn toward the area near the dirt road where the barn had stood. A high mesh fence enclosed a large square. As we approached the fence we could see that a tennis court had replaced the barn. We stood for a minute looking through the fence.

"I wish we had never come up here," Jack said.

"Jack, what's the matter? You look so sad."

"Annie, did you ever wonder why Aunt Belle and Uncle Ivan didn't come back to live in Brooklyn after the farm was sold?"

"No, I never thought about it," I said. It had never occurred to me that there was any particular reason why our family remained in Brooklyn and Ivan's family moved to Liberty.

Jack started to walk around the fence, and I followed him, grasping the mesh wire to keep from sliding on the crisp snow. When we came to the far side of the court, Jack stopped.

"Did you know there was a small door right about here at the back of the barn?" he said. "Harry and I used to get into the barn that way. There was a narrow footpath from the road."

"Harry? Your friend Harry Standig?"

"We were very clever. We used to go past the barn to the road and come in through the back."

"I didn't know anyone could get into the barn. The big front doors were boarded up weren't they? And there was no path through all that nasty stuff growing around it. There must have been snakes, and rats, and gophers in that scrub grass."

"You're right. That's why Harry and I were so glad to discover the footpath off the road and the little back door."

"What did you want to go into the barn for? What was in there?"

"Nothing much. There were a few stalls on one side, probably for horses or cows. The rest of the place was empty. There was a skylight. The floor was dirt with sawdust over it."

"What did you do in there? It sounds creepy to me."

"We were exploring," he said with a hint of a smile.

"Exploring?"

"The delights of the flesh. Harry's brother gave us a dirty book and some Playboys. We stashed them in a pail in one of the stalls, and we'd go there about once a week to read and look at the pictures."

A sharp wind came up and the sky darkened.

"We should start back," Jack said. "It's going to snow again." We went back to the car.

"That isn't the end of the story, is it? You wanted to tell me something more."

"You're right," he said. He started the engine and drove slowly over the tracks we had made earlier.

"Harry and I went to the barn one night, about nine o'clock. It was the first time we'd gone there at night. We were sitting on the floor in one of the stalls, reading by flashlight, when we heard the back door open."

"Is this one of your dumb ghost stories?" I said.

"No, Annie. Just listen. We clicked off our lights and sat very still. Somebody came in and closed the door. We were scared out of our wits. I peeked around the edge of the stall. The moon was shining in through the skylight, and I saw a man spreading a blanket on the floor. Harry leaned over me to see. A minute later, somebody else came in.

"The man said, 'Good, I thought you wouldn't come.'

"Then there was a woman's voice. She said, 'I didn't want to. I came to tell you we have to stop this.' And the man yelled, real loud and rough, 'No!' The woman started to cry."

"Who were they?" I said.

Jack took a deep breath. "She got hysterical. She was begging him, saying things like, 'Let me go…the children.' And he said 'I'll never let you go.'

"I saw the man reach for her, and they struggled a little. Then they were on the blanket on the ground."

"Jack, who were those people?"

"I pushed Harry back," he said, "and we leaned against the side of the stall, listening to their sounds. After a half hour, we heard the door creak open, and they left."

"Jack, for heaven's sake, who were they?"

"Don't you know?"

I turned to look at him. He gazed straight ahead, his hands tight on the wheel. His cheek twitched.

"Harry and I left the barn. He never did tell me if he recognized the voices of Mama and Uncle Ivan. I suspect that he did because he never mentioned it. Good old Harry. We didn't go to the barn again the rest of the summer."

As we sped toward New York City, I was caught in the mesmerizing beat of the tires, my heart stung by the insult to my comfortable memories.

The street was dark under a frigid moon when we pulled up in front of my apartment building. Jack placed my suitcase on the pavement and embraced me, pressing his cheek to mine. "I'm sorry, Annie," he said. "I had to tell you. I've needed to tell someone for so long."

He slid into his car and drove away.

That night, unable to sleep, I stood at my window and looked up at the sky where a meteor raced across the dark expanse and faded into dust.

LITTLE DOVE

Avram Silber was a prudent man. He stood on the crowded ferry dock, reached into his oversized coat, and massaged the lump of American bills, thirty dollars worth, sewn into the lining of his jacket. He lifted his woolen cap and stroked his bald head—a nervous habit that helped him to think. His neck muscles contracted in the cool October air. Beside him, his daughter clutched a woolen shawl under her chin. It pleased Avram to know that Raisle, also, had two American dollars sewn into her bodice waist several layers beneath her outer coat. Never mind that he had been cheated by that thief on board the ship who had charged him a ruble to change his money.

The trials of their trip in steerage across the ocean on the S.S. Hamburg and the torturous immigration procedures at Ellis Island pressed on him. They had been examined like a pair of carp in the market. Doctors had prodded their mouths open and projected lights into their noses and eyes and ears. They had been questioned by a crew of dispassionate officials. The questions had frightened and baffled them. "Who is receiving you in the United States? Do you have a criminal record? Do you have a job? Is there any mental illness in your family? How much money do you have?"

Avram had to make a fast decision. Should he tell how much money? Is it better to have more, or less? He calculated his American dollars and his kopecks and told them. Even their bags had been opened and scrutinized before they were permitted to disembark at New York harbor. They stood now on the pier dazed and immobile with their belongings at their feet. A small green park showed through the skeleton of an elevated railway at the end of the pier.

Avram looked across the throngs of their compatriots on the pier to the street beyond. When he shifted his weight on the wooden planks of the dock, his remaining kopecks, thirty of them, jangled in his pockets and spurred him to action.

"Come, Raisle," he said. "We'll go on the other side."

"Papa, they told us to wait here."

"I'm tired of waiting and waiting," he said with a glance at the ferry building. His resentment of the ship's authorities had not softened even after they gave him his sister's address, written in English, on a yellow paper. He checked his breast pocket under his bulging coat for the slip of paper. It was there. He patted the pocket twice.

Avram used his large wicker suitcase to open a path through the crowd while Raisle, the taller of the two, followed carrying a carpet bag and a featherbed bound with rope suspended from her shoulder. They passed under the elevated railway, walked a few blocks and stopped at a corner. Midway down the street a sign "Money Changer" printed in English, Yiddish, and Russian jutted out toward the curb. The sidewalk traffic was thick. Avram tugged at Raisle's elbow and stationed her near a frankfurter vendor who did a lively business from his cart.

"Stand right here," he said, "and don't talk to anyone until I come back." He placed his suitcase beside her.

"Papa, I'm afraid." Raisle looked with apprehension at the people who flowed down the street in the rhythm of an army of ants.

"*Shah*," Avram said. "I won't be long. Just keep your eyes on me and watch where I'm going."

He passed a pawnbroker, and a sidewalk stall selling men's suits and shoes. An overhead sign on a doorway announced, "Rabbi Eleazer Glick—Marriages Performed." Next door, scrawled in black paint across the grimy storefront window were the words "Slutsky—Money Changer." Avram entered the long narrow store. A man sat before a rickety table eating a piece of black bread and dried fish. He sipped tea from a glass. Nobody else was in the store. The man waved his bread toward a row of wooden crates against the wall. Avram sat down.

When Slutsky finished his meal, he expelled a loud belch and set his glass of tea aside. He jerked his head at Avram who approached, gathering the kopecks from his pocket. Avram placed them on the table. Slutsky smiled broadly. "Ah, a *landsman*," he said. They negotiated in Russian, and Avram picked up his American money. Avram learned from Slutsky that he could get a wagon cart on this same street that would take him to his sister's house.

He hurried back toward the corner where he had left his daughter. Raisle was eating something, while a woman stood before her talking and gesturing. The woman wore a brown coat with a mangy fur collar open at the neck and a low cut orange dress. Her skin was the color of coffee with cream. Avram noted that the hems of both the dress and coat were well above her ankles. A beaded headband held a green plume in her kinky hair that was the same orange color as her dress.

"What's going on here?" he said to his daughter. "Who is this…this…?" his words clogged in his throat as if a raw potato was stuck in his mouth.

Raisle took a huge bite of a frankfurter that she held in both hands. "This lady bought this for me." She turned toward the frankfurter stand. "I was so hungry," she mumbled, still chewing. "People were buying this food, and it smelled so good." Avram glared at the vendor.

"What were you talking about with this woman?"

"I don't know, Papa. I couldn't understand, but I think she wanted me to go with her."

"Aye!" Avram yelled. He turned to the woman and shoved her with the back of his hand. "Get away from my girl," he shouted in Russian.

The woman smiled, revealing a large gold tooth, and with a toss of her head, she moved back. Before turning away, she blew a kiss in Raisle's direction and lifted a dollar bill from between her breasts, waved it with two fingers, and returned it to its place.

"What were you thinking?" Avram screamed at his daughter. "Don't you know what that woman is?"

Raisle stared at him, her blue eyes wide open, as she chewed the last of the frankfurter, and sucked the sauerkraut off her fingers. Her shawl had fallen back and her pale brown hair lay in a cascade over her collar. He was struck by her vulnerability.

"You will not talk to anyone until we get to Teible's house," he blustered. "I thought you were a smart girl, but you're a goose...a goose...Don't you know what could..."

The sound of a horse cart rattling down the cobbled street interrupted his ranting. He jumped in front of the startled horse and waved his yellow paper at the driver. In a few minutes, they were aboard the cart, baggage and featherbed at their feet on the slatted floor.

Raisle held the yellow slip of paper. "Teible," she said. "What a lovely name your sister has...Teible, little dove. Is she really a little dove?"

Avram did not answer. He looked straight ahead.

They bounced through a stand of tenements that rose on both sides of the dusty streets. Laundry hung from the fire-escapes. Globs of horse manure and assorted trash lay on the streets and in the gutters. A steady stream of people moved along the sidewalks, crossing with indifference in the path of the horse carts and pushcarts.

They rode until dusk. Avram ate a hard heel of bread with an onion which he brought out of his overcoat pocket. Eventually, the cart turned a corner, and they rode down a grand street of two story brick houses, all attached, with porches on the lower floors. The cart stopped before 242 Browne Street, and they unloaded their baggage on the cracked pavement.

Raisle looked up at the house. "How do you know they want us?" she said. "They didn't come to the boat."

"Maybe they didn't get my letter," he said. "What are you worried about? Teible is my sister. She used to take care of me when I was a baby."

"You haven't seen her for ten years. Maybe she doesn't want us."

"Of course, she wants us. What are you talking about?" He started to carry the baggage toward the porch.

A window on the upper floor screeched open and a woman leaned out. "What's going on there? Who's there?" she yelled.

"Teible? Teible, it's me Avram. I came from Minsk. I'm here."

A minute passed, and the window slammed shut. Avram glanced at his daughter who looked frozen with foreboding. When the wooden door to the house swung open, Avram jumped. His sister Teible filled the door frame. She waved a newspaper at them.

"It said tomorrow," she complained. "In the paper... 'SS Hamburg will arrive Monday, October 30, 1905.' That's tomorrow."

"I don't know," Avram stammered. "The boat docked in the harbor. I don't know what day it is."

A raucous male laugh floated down a long narrow stairway behind her. Teible closed the door and came out onto the porch. A cotton checked dress covered her two hundred pound rectangle of a body. Her thick dark hair was drawn back in a bun from a center part. Thick eyebrows spanned the bridge of her nose. A large mole on her chin sprouted three jaunty black hairs.

"All right. So, come on the porch," Teible said. "Avram, you look the same." Her gaze shifted past him to Raisle who had picked up her featherbed and clutched it like a shield against her body. "So that's Raisle. What's the matter with you, girl? Come here. Come on the porch." She extended an arm, and Raisle ascended the four steps, still holding her featherbed.

"She's so skinny," Teible said. "Avrum, how old is she?"

Raisle glanced at her father who gave her an encouraging nod.

"I'm sixteen, *Tante* Teible," she murmured.

The door opened again, and a short man about half the size of Teible in width and weight came out. Teible went to the far end of the porch, and the man followed. They conferred in whispers for a minute. The man cast an anxious look at the newcomers and went inside.

"That's Dovid, my husband," she said to Avram.

"Ah, yes, you wrote me that you got married."

"He's no prize, but he makes a living...Listen, we'll go upstairs, but we have to wait a minute. You're hungry?"

They were silent for a time, each absorbed in thought. Avram removed his hat and swabbed his damp head with a handkerchief. The lump in the lining of his jacket afforded him a merciful sense of security.

Again, the door opened, and eight men came out and passed one by one down the steps to the sidewalk. A few of them stopped to put their coats on and turned and glared at Teible and then dispersed in different directions down the street.

"Come. Come upstairs," Teible said.

They carried the baggage one flight up. Dovid stood in the doorway that opened into a large kitchen, where an enameled table was covered with platters of cakes and cookies and a huge bowl of chick peas. Several bottles of liquor and seltzer stood in a row. Dovid immediately started to clear the table. "We were having a little party," he said with a shrug.

"All right, Dovid. At least say hello to my brother Avrum and his girl." Turning to Avram, "He's such a fool," she said. "He don't even know how to behave with people."

Avram shook hands with his brother-in-law whose face had turned red. Dovid's watery blue eyes were pink-rimmed, and his thinning hair ran in disarray over his pate. His shoulders turned inward as if for protection. Poor man, Avram thought.

Another large room off the kitchen was almost bare except for four card tables in the middle and two narrow cots covered with flowered spreads standing head to foot along one wall. Teible called this room "the parlor." She seated Avram and Raisle at one of the card tables, and in five minutes, emerged from the kitchen with two plates of borsht with meat, and thick slices of dark bread. Avram ate with intensity, and when he wiped up the last bit of soup with his bread, he saw that Raisle had not touched her food. In his daughter's face, he saw a familiar look—rebelliousness and growing resolve. He knew her throat was clogged, holding back a well of tears.

Avram and Raisle slept on the cots in the parlor. In the morning, Avram swung his feet onto the cold linoleum floor when he heard Raisle stirring.

"Did you sleep well, daughter?" he said.

She sat up and shivered scratching the small of her back. "I think I shared my cot with bedbugs. And I was cold," she whispered. She had not used her featherbed because it was too large for the narrow cot.

Teible in a flannel robe appeared in the kitchen doorway. Her hair hung loose. Without her corset, her girth had ballooned like a giant melon. "Good. You're awake," she said. Come in the kitchen." She served them bowls of rice with hot milk and butter and went to the stove to boil coffee and chicory in a saucepan.

"So what do you think to do?" she said. She poured coffee and milk into three glasses and spooned three teaspoons of sugar in each. "Dovid could get you work, Avram, on Hester Street. He's there now with his pushcart."

"What kind of work?"

"Pushcart work. What do you think? Dovid can show you where to rent a cart and how to find a place on the street."

Avram looked into his bowl. "In Minsk I had a little store—yard goods—wool and cotton, and even silk. But the Cossacks came and broke my window. I thought…"

"What's the matter? You're too swell for a pushcart? Maybe you have money to open up a fancy store…Well, you have money?"

"No," Avram said. "What could I sell on a pushcart?

"Anything you want. You'll talk to Dovid tonight." She turned her attention to Raisle. "So what can you do, girl? You know how to cook?"

"I learned a little from my mother before she died."

"Good. I can use you."

"Papa, you told me I could go to school in America."

"School?" Teible shrieked. "School is for rich people. Forget about such nonsense. You'll be with us. Avram, you'll work and save up some money. Maybe you can open a store sometime. School," she sneered.

She stared at Raisle with a frown. "What are you doing, girl? Can't you sit still?"

Raisle had pulled her nightgown sleeves up and had been scratching her inner arms where long streaks appeared over tiny red dots. Teible took her wrist and pulled her arm outward to see.

"Aye, the *vantsen*! Later I'll give you some Flit to spray your bed."

Avram and Raisle signed up for conversational English given twice a week at the Hebrew Educational Society in a ramshackle old house, once the domain of a wealthy family. Avram went to work on Hester Street selling sundries from a pushcart. He carried buttons, needles and pins, shoelaces, combs, razors, and scissors. His pushcart, new on the street, was slow to take hold. After a month, he barely earned enough to pay Teible for room and board.

Raisle was put to work cooking and cleaning in the four room flat. Twice a week, on Sundays and Wednesdays, she helped serve the men who came to Teible's to play pinochle on the tables in the parlor. On Friday nights Dovid brought home from his pushcart a huge bushel of spoiled fruit that could not be sold. Teible and Raisle worked into the night cutting away the rotted parts and saving the rest for baking the next day.

The rabbi who lived in the flat beneath them would shake his fist at Dovid when he came down to the tin garbage cans in front of the house. "*Goyim*—cooking and working on *Shabbus*. No respect for God's holy day!"

On Saturdays, Teible and Raisle baked the cakes and prepared huge pots of chick peas that had to be soaked and boiled for hours. They made knishes and other snacks to be served with the whiskey that the pinochle players downed from shot glasses. The money for each shot was placed in a sugar bowl that soon filled up. Sometimes, a wife or girlfriend came to kibitz. The noise in the room muffled the periodic pounding under the floor made by the rabbi's broomstick poking up on his ceiling. Once the rabbi called the police who came and had some wine and honeycake. The games continued. The players paid Teible a dollar each as they filed out of the flat to go home.

On a Friday afternoon in December, Raisle put on her coat and went down the stairs with a bag of garbage. She didn't come back.

After searching the neighborhood, Avram returned to the flat at midnight and stationed himself at the window for the remainder of the night looking through the cold window pane at the deserted street below. At six, Teible came out of her room.

"I'll call the police," Avram said.

"Police? No police…she'll come back," Teible said. "Believe me, she'll get hungry. She'll come back and beg to be taken in. No police. How could she do this to me? I treated her like a princess. She ate like a queen—like a queen, I tell you—all the best. The trouble is she doesn't like to work. That's what the trouble is."

Avram glared at his sister. "She doesn't even have her shawl with her." He put on his coat and hat. "I'm going out to look for her."

He started on the same path the horse cart had taken when it brought them from New York Harbor. Where else would she go? he thought. Where else would she know? The harbor was not that far—maybe two or three miles.

He walked in the morning darkness and prayed to a long abandoned entity that it would not snow. If I find her, he told himself and that "other," I promise I will go to *shul* every day and give a substantial donation. I will become a pillar, upright and pious. Please, let it not snow…please, let me find her.

The corner on State Street where they had stood that first day looked vacant, unfamiliar. There were few people, and the frankfurter stand was absent. He could see the tops of the trees in the park through the skeleton of the elevated railway. The sparse gray leaves shivered as a train rattled by. He stopped a man walking down the street and asked the time. Eight-fifteen. He passed the pawnbroker, Rabbi Glick's door, and Slutsky's, not open yet. In a luncheonette, he sat at the counter and bought a cup of coffee and a roll. Across the street, a greens store was opening for the day. Good, he thought. At least she can find food. He knew she still carried the two American dollars in her bodice waist. He took his time to finish his meal, for he had no plan.

Avram walked back to the corner. The red-headed negress was crossing toward him. As soon as she saw him, she stopped in the middle of the street, turned, and started to run toward the pier. Avrum watched her for a few seconds until it dawned on him that that crazy woman knew where Raisle was. He started after her. She twisted to look at him as she ran and increased her speed. They raced into the park. She zigzagged between some trees, and ran behind a long hedge and disappeared.

He circled the park several times and sat on a bench next to a bearded young man. A small trunk bound with a leather strap was at the man's feet, and three large bunches of bananas were on the seat next to him. Despite the cold, his hat was set back on his dark hair, the brim curling upward. He had no overcoat. He clutched the collar of his jacket under his chin with his chapped, red hand. The man gave a speculative look at Avram. "Maybe you want to buy some bananas?" he said in English.

Avram recognized in the dark mournful eyes the unmistakable mark transported down through a millennium of Hebrews. So, he replied in Yiddish. "*A shainem dank*—No, thanks."

The man's face brightened, and he reached out and clasped Avram's hand with both of his like a hug. "Ah, thank God… one of ours!" he said. "My name is Levin, Alexei Levin. I came Friday from Russia…Vilna."

"Avram Silber, from Minsk." Their hands remained clasped while they eyed one another. "Why are you here selling bananas?"

"Ah, it's a story, but I'll tell you." He shifted in his seat and looked at the ground as he spoke. "I came across two days ago on a ship from Amsterdam. We had bad storms, winds…it was terrible. We sailed for twenty-nine days. They ran out of food. I had to buy from passengers who brought their own food—potatoes—pickled cabbage—sausages. By the time we landed, I had only three kopecks. I didn't know what to do." He hunched his shoulders against a sudden wind. "At the end of the pier," he continued, "another ship was unloading bananas. Some men asked me if I wanted a job. I worked a full day unloading bananas. When I finished, they didn't give me money. They gave me half a hand of bananas. I couldn't do anything. Those men...They said I could sell the bananas. I ate a few of them. Yesterday, two ships came into the harbor, so I sold some."

He shivered and crossed his arms to rub warmth into them. He looked around the deserted park. "There is no ship today."

"Where have you been staying?" Avram said.

He hesitated. "I've been sleeping on a bench in the barge house. I am embarrassed by my stupidity."

"What are you going to do now?"

"I don't know. I don't have enough to buy a ticket to Charlotte. That's a city where my cousin lives. At first, I wanted to remain in New York. I thought I could get a job here and maybe find a nice wife. But, I don't like it here. It's too cold." His eyes, extra large in his gaunt face, were watery.

"What kind of work do you do?"

"I'm a teacher. In Vilna, I taught in a Russian school."

"A Jew in a Russian school?"

"I think they didn't know. Sometimes I worked on *Shabbus*."

Through his own anxiety, Avram ached for this young man in whom he perceived a depth of character and intelligence.

"I have to go now. I'll buy a banana."

Levin snapped a banana off a bunch. "It's a gift to you. It has been a pleasure to talk to a kindred person."

Avram walked back to State Street. It was around noon. The frankfurter vendor was there doing a brisk business. Down the street, Slutsky's was open, and Avram went in to borrow a wooden crate so that he could sit on the corner and wait.

"Maybe you remember me?" Avram said. "I'm a *landsman* from Minsk."

Slutsky was dealing with a customer. "Take a seat," he said pointing to the row of crates against the wall. When the customer left, Slutsky said, "So, what can I do for a *landsman*? You need more American dollars?"

"I came to ask if I could borrow one of your crates for a couple of hours."

"For what do you need one of my crates?"

Avram swallowed hard and to his surprise began to cry. The story, beginning at his arrival on the S. S. Hamburg, to his reception at Teible's house, to the disappearance of his daughter, to his bizarre run-in with the negress, spilled out in a torrent of sobs. Slutsky's hard mask of a face softened.

"That woman…does she have red hair?"

Avram's eyes opened wide. He nodded.

"That's Fritzie, the *courveh*. Everyone knows her. She does her business on this street. Whenever a ship comes in to the harbor, she's here, walking up and down looking for men and new women for her business."

Avram wiped his eyes and stared into Slutsky's face.

"I'll tell you what, my friend," Slutsky continued. "Stay here with me. She passes my store almost every day. I know she lives in a hotel on Broadway. I don't know the name, but Broadway is a few blocks from here…Come, sit down. I'll make some tea."

It was two-thirty when Fritzie passed Slutsky's store, arm-in-arm with a sailor. Avram slipped into his coat and shook Slutskey's hand.

"Come back later. I live in a room behind the store. Go…go before you lose her," Slutsky said. "And good luck!"

Avram followed close behind the pair, since the sidewalks now were active with people. They crossed several streets, walking at a steady pace, turned a corner, and entered a red brick building. A sign over the door under an ornate arch said, "Hotel Ambassador."

When Avram entered, he faced an eight foot long desk with a wall of cubicles behind it. Fritzie and the sailor were not in the room. A carpeted stairway rose on the left. A huge man in shirtsleeves sat behind the desk. Avram almost swooned from the sudden warmth of the room and the rancid smell of a stale cigar in a chipped saucer on the desk. The man looked up from a newspaper.

Avram said in English, "Where is the woman Fritzie?"

The man examined Avram down and up and smiled. "I'm sorry," he said with a tilt of his head toward the stairway, "but she's spoken for right now."

Avram wasn't sure what the words meant, but he did recognize the denial.

"I want Raisle." His voice rose. "The young girl, Raisle. She is here, no?"

The man chuckled. "Hold your water, mister. Relax." He opened a door behind him. "Mrs. Reardon, would you step out here for a moment."

Mrs. Reardon, a middle-aged woman in a purple dress over a hefty corseted body, stepped into the room. Her black hair was pasted to her face in marcelled waves.

"I want Raisle," Avram said on the verge of tears.

Mrs. Reardon glanced at the man behind the counter, eyebrows raised in a show of amusement. "I take it you mean 'Roselle'," she said. "She's new here. This is her first day. How did you hear about her?"

"I don't know." His voice cracked. "Where is she?" His eyes spanned the lobby, and he started toward the staircase. The man came around the counter and grabbed Avram by the back of his collar. "Just a minute, old timer. Take it easy."

Mrs. Reardon hooked her arm in Avram's, and they forced him into an upholstered chair.

"If you'll just relax, I'll see what I can do," Mrs. Reardon said. "She's new, so you'll have to calm down."

Avram got the sense of what she was saying and leaned back in the chair.

Mrs. Reardon exchanged a few hushed words and laughs with the man at the desk. She beckoned Avram to follow her. As they walked up the stairway, she said, "The price is usually fifty

cents, but Roselle's a virgin, so it will cost you a dollar. Okay?"
She turned to look at him.

At the top of the stairs, they turned into a large room furnished
with a brocade sofa and three upholstered chairs. Two women sat
on the sofa, one about twenty-five, dressed in street clothes. Her
companion was about forty, wearing a flimsy kimono. Avram
stood frozen in the middle of the room facing the door. He dared
not look at the women, although he could hear them whispering
and giggling.

The sound of voices came through the transom. Mrs. Reardon
was arguing with someone. He opened the door. Mrs. Reardon
was holding Raisle by the wrist and they were tugging at
Raisle's wool coat. Raisle was wearing a blue dress he had not
seen before.

"Just meet him, Roselle. He's willing to pay a dollar," Mrs.
Reardon yelled.

"Raisle!" Avram cried.

"Papa!"

The coat landed on the floor and Avram picked it up and
grabbed Raisle's arm in one motion. A vision of Mrs. Reardon's
outraged face followed him as they raced down the steps and out
the front door. At the corner, they stopped, and Raisle slipped
her arms into the coat. They started to walk.

"What were you thinking? How could you do this?"

"They said I would be a maid...to keep the rooms clean and
help the ladies."

"Ladies? You call them ladies?"

"They gave me this dress. They were kind to me and made
me laugh."

"They wanted to sell you to me for a dollar!" He jerked her
arm. "Why? Why did God punish me with such a daughter?"

They walked in silence for a minute.

"I'm not going back to Teible," Raisle announced.

"You'll go where I tell you to go!"

Raisle stopped walking. That look rose in her face—stubborn and guarded. Avram grabbed her arm and pulled her down the street toward the trees at Battery Park. He increased his pace and dragged his daughter in a run after him. In the park, he headed straight for the bench. Alexei Levin was still there, two bunches of bananas beside him. Avram forced Raisle down on the bench and stood before them.

"Alexei? That's your name, Alexei Levin?"

The young man nodded.

"How old are you, Alexei Levin?

Alexei's smile faded, and he glanced at Raisle beside him.

"I'm twenty-two," he said.

"You've never been married?"

"No, of course not. What's happening?"

Avram lifted his hat and brushed the top of his head with his palm.

"Come, we'll take a walk," he said. "This is Raisle, my daughter." He picked up the bananas. "Come. You won't be sorry."

They walked out of the park three abreast, Avram in the middle, Alexei lugging his trunk by the leather strap, and Raisle every minute shrugging off her father's grasp on her arm. Avram talked, directing his questions to Alexei Levin.

They learned that Alexei's father had been an Englishman and had come to Russia to join the Marxist communists. He died of a heart attack when Alexei was fourteen. Alexei lived with his mother in Vilna until she died of consumption when he was eighteen. Two years later he went to work at the Russian school. One day, government officials came to the school to seek candidates for conscription in the army. They took his name. Alexei did not report for work the next day. Instead he traveled to Amsterdam where he made arrangements to sail to America.

"A Jew in the Russian army..." he explained with a shrug. "What would have become of me?"

Avram led them into the luncheonette on State Street, where they sat at a small table and ordered bowls of soup. They sat in silence for several minutes, the energy of animated thought swimming around them. Avram crossed his arms on the table and leaned forward.

"I have a proposition for you, Alexei Levin," he said. "I have thirty American dollars here in my coat. I will give them to you if you will take my daughter with you to Charlotte."

"Papa!" Raisle rasped in a whisper.

"*Shah*…You have nothing to say about this."

Raisle's eyes now were fixed on the table. The waiter brought the soup and black bread.

"There is a rabbi on the next block who can perform the marriage," Avram continued. "Raisle is a good girl, only sixteen, but very intelligent. She is healthy and a good cook." Avram turned to look at his daughter. "She is pretty, no?"

"Papa!" Raisle said. She stood up.

Avram pulled her back in her seat. "You have a choice," he said. "Go with this fine young man, or come with me back to Teible." He looked from one to the other. "You should think a bit…and talk." He rose and went to the counter. Taking a stool near the door, he turned his back to them.

After a few minutes, Avram glanced their way. The soup on the table was untouched. Raisle's head was lowered and Alexei was talking to her. Avram could not hear his words, but Raisle looked up. She was listening.

Fifteen minutes passed. Avram observed the couple. There was a blush on Raisle's cheeks. The look of anxiety that had dwelt in Alexei's face from the first moment of their meeting was gone.

At six-thirty P.M. they walked up a flight of stairs to Rabbi Glick's quarters. The ceremony took less than five minutes. The rabbi's wife, wearing an apron over her cotton dress, stood in the doorway of his study. Avram asked for a pair of scissors. He removed the roll of American dollars from its place in his jacket lining.

Outside, they waited in the dusk for a horse cart to take the couple to the railroad station. They wrote addresses on scraps of paper. Avram took a deep breath. He felt an aura of tranquility hovering over them like the gentle flutter of a little dove.

Their eyes turned toward the rattle of a bright red horse cart coming toward them. They exchanged kisses and handshakes. Avram's gaze followed the cart as it carried his daughter and her husband away.

"Papa," Raisle called, standing up in the cart. "Alexei has promised to teach me to read and write English." Avram walked down the street toward Slutsky's—perhaps for a glass of tea.

CHANGES

When Harry came home from work, reeking of industrial paint and benzene, there was no supper cooking. Leah was on the floor in their bedroom with her arms covering her head. The doctor came and said that the nervous sickness was from her "changes." Leah did not understand. "What does it mean... changes?" she said.

Dr. Markoff closed his medical bag. "We're all getting older, Leah. You're fifty-two. You're not a spring chicken anymore. Your body is changing." He wrote a prescription. "I'll come to see you tomorrow," he said.

Leah turned on her side in the bed and looked out the window. The only changes she was aware of had come with creeping steadiness over the years, invoking memories now—Molly's sparkling baby giggle, little Philip's soft brown curls, the sweet hot smell of Benjy when he came home from the schoolyard, panting, with his roller skates slung over his skinny shoulder—memories all shimmering in the past.

It was new and strange the way the family attended her when she was sick. When Molly came home from work, she took over the cooking of supper, and Harry brought food in from the grocery and put everything in the refrigerator. The boys were quiet in the house. Benjy went out each morning before leaving for school and bought her the DAILY FORWARD, and Phil made her a glass of tea when he came home from the hardware store where he worked. They even sent the sheets out to the Chinaman on the next block. But, Leah distrusted the alien smell of the boiled sheets and the wooden feel of them folded stiff around a gray cardboard.

Leah went back with ease to her regular chores—washing, ironing, cooking. Her routine included the Sunday nights of her wifely duty under the weight of her husband with his dapple-gray winter underwear thumping on her chest. Harry wore this underwear winter and summer. She held a suit of it now in her hands and rubbed it against the washboard in a tub of suds. This washboard was the same one she had brought with her from Europe when she was a bride of nineteen. The metal ridges no longer infringed on her knuckles. Her hands had become cal-lused over the past thirty-three years.

On this December morning, a pleasant thought accompanied her scrubbing. Her Molly would be married to Walter Garber on Thursday in the rabbi's study, and a party would be held for the immediate relatives and neighbors that same evening in the family's five-room flat. Leah would have to squeeze her chores to make time to remove the plastic slipcover from the sofa, to take down and wash the curtains in the parlor, and to organize the menu for the party.

Sarah, her neighbor, whose husband owned a pickle business, would provide the sours. Harry would go to a special store down-town for the lox and bagels. The challah had been ordered from the bakery, and Leah would cook the *gefilte* fish—six pounds of carp and yellow pike already on order at the market.

Walter's mother would bake the honey cake and sponge cake.

"At least she can do that much," Harry complained. "By rights, she should provide the schnapps."

"Harry…Harry, be a *mensch*," Leah said. "She's a poor widow. We have plenty of schnapps and wine left over from the seder."

"At least she could have offered," Harry said.

Leah would have to find a way to get some extra money out of Harry. True, it was easier now that she had the nervous sickness—she was still taking the pills Dr. Markoff had prescribed. Harry was gentler, now, when he spoke to her. But, she didn't dare tell him how much the fish cost, especially since she was paying extra to have it filleted.

Leah wrung out the last item of wash and placed it on a mound of tightly rolled pieces in a basin. She wiped her brow with a kitchen towel and sat down at the table to rest and read the newspaper.

One of her few pleasures was the advice column in the DAILY FORWARD. She turned to the *Bintel Brief*, squinting at the curly letters of the Hebrew alphabet. The content was disappointing today—whining letters having to do with soldiers and wives—a mother who despaired about her son not writing, and a wife who complained that her husband's military allotment check was being dispatched to her mother-in-law.

Leah had a detached association with the events of the war. Phil, who was twenty-one, had been designated 4F by the Draft Board because of his myopia, and Benjy was not yet eighteen. She had no idea what work Molly did at the defense plant. A portion of Molly's salary was turned over to her father for room and board, as he called it. What was left she spent on subway fare and the mysterious frivolities of young women.

The only personal trouble Leah had encountered, because of the war, was the fact that most of the marriageable boys in the neighborhood had been called up. Her Molly was twenty-three. But now she was engaged.

Leah recalled the June evening when Molly had come into the house breathless and animated. "Guess who I met in the candy store?" she said. "Walter Garber. He's home on leave."

"I remember him," Leah said. "He was the boy with all those pimples."

"He has no pimples, now. He looks so good in that army uniform. He asked me for a date. We're going to the movies tomorrow."

Molly and Walter met every night that week, which gave Leah a reason to hope. When Walter returned to Camp Dix, a busy correspondence began between them. A letter for Molly arrived every day. Each evening when Molly came home from work, she would pick her letter up from the kitchen table, hold it against her chest, and rush like a squirrel into her room. Leah was fascinated by a conspicuous change in her. Molly's sullen expression turned softer as if there were a smile concealed in her.

The wedding plans came six months later after Molly took her daily letter to her room. In five minutes, she came back into the kitchen holding the letter. Leah was serving Harry his soup.

"Walter is coming in for another leave," Molly announced. "Ten days." There was a light in her eyes. "He wants us to get married while he's home."

Before Leah could blurt out her happiness, Harry turned in his seat.

"What's the big hurry? Maybe you didn't hear there's a war on?"

"Papa, after this leave, Walter is going to be shipped overseas."

"That's all the more reason you should wait."

"Harry," Leah said. "What's the matter with you? How many more chances will she get? Why shouldn't they get married now?"

"Papa, we love each other."

"When is he coming in?" Harry asked. "We can talk about it then."

"He's coming in Saturday," Molly said. "There's nothing to talk about. We're getting married."

The two women's eyes were fixed on him. He stood up and went to look out the window. "I don't see what's the hurry," he mumbled.

That night, as Leah and Harry prepared for bed, he said, "Walter's mother—she's a widow. Does that mean I have to pay for everything?"

Leah smiled. There would be a wedding.

Rising from the kitchen table, Leah brought the basin of damp laundry to the bedroom where she set it on a chair and opened the window to a gust of icy air. She hung the shirts and underwear with wooden pins on the cold hard rope that stretched on a pulley to a window in another tenement across the courtyard. When she was done, she called across to the neighboring flat, "Sarah...Sarah." The window opened, and a heavy woman, wearing a bulky red sweater, leaned out.

Leah called, "Are you going to the Rialto tonight?"

"Of course, what then?" Sarah replied. "It's the last soup dish they're giving tonight. Do you have the whole set?"

Leah nodded. "All except the last soup dish. What's playing tonight?"

"I don't know," Sarah said. "I'll meet you downstairs in the hall. Seven o'clock."

Late that night when she heard Harry snoring beside her, Leah got out of bed, moved to the closet, and slid a heavy corrugated carton out onto the linoleum floor. She opened the box and removed the top layer of newspaper. Satisfaction softened her face as she examined the last soup dish in this service for eight, her wedding present for Molly. She ran a finger around the border of the dish, circling the delicate blue and red flowers on the edge. She closed the box, slid it back into the closet and returned to bed.

After the ceremony in Rabbi Nussbaum's study, ten members of the wedding party, in pairs and threes, walked several blocks to the apartment. It occurred to Leah as they walked that she had heard but a few of the solemn words of the ceremony. She was happy but uneasy. Something troubled her, a shapeless disturbance that she could not grab hold of.

It was four o'clock and the guests were to arrive at five. The folding tables were already set up end to end in the middle of the parlor, the sofa and chairs pushed back to the wall. Molly removed her veiled hat and her new mouton lamb jacket and put on an apron. Leah and Molly spread a white cloth over the tables.

Leah observed Harry as he arranged the wine and schnapps on the buffet. He was a good man, aloof and distant but not unkind. His connection with the children when they were small consisted of fumbling overtures of affection—a pat on the head, a pinch on the cheek.

Leah watched him open a box of cigars and place it on one end of the table. She knew that he had another box held aside for his friends at Diamond's Cafeteria. Each Sunday, he took a bus to Diamond's where he had a pastry and several glasses of tea throughout the day while sitting at a table arguing politics with his cronies.

Harry's graying hair was plastered down now for this occasion. A printed tie, with a clumsy knot, hung below his waist where his white shirt protested the tight fit over his paunch. Molly went to help him lay out the glasses and Walter's mother unveiled her platter of cake. Walter went down to the candy store to call the hired hack to make sure he would be on time, eight P. M., to drive him and his bride to the Palace Hotel in Lakewood, N. J., for their four day honeymoon.

Leah tugged at her blue dress, the same one she had worn to all the family functions for the past five years. Her face was powdered and rouged and felt stiff like an eggshell. The night before, Molly had rolled Leah's dark hair up in curlers. Her daughter had stood behind her, both of them gazing into the mirror. When Molly was little, they had shared their small world. It had been easy then. But now, time had spread an unbridgeable gap between them. Leah had been too comfortable in the embrace of her household responsibilities. Molly had advanced with the changing times, pulling ahead of her, leaving Leah behind, marooned in her insular life.

Leah felt an overwhelming regret and sadness. She had not had the courage to penetrate the scary world out there. She looked with expectation at Molly's reflection in the mirror. Their eyes met, but neither of them said anything. The moment was lost.

Leah was fussing over the platter of fish when she looked up and saw her daughter staring at her. Molly started to speak, but the doorbell rang. The first guests had arrived, and Molly went to greet them.

Thirty people crowded into the small flat. A few children, dressed in their Sabbath clothes, scooted in and out among the guests. Harry's brother, Max, brought his accordion, and after two songs, was dismissed by the group. "Such a noise!" Walter's mother said. The guests carried their paper plates through the rooms as if in a maze.

Upon the inevitable calls of "Speech, speech," Phil stood against a wall and raised his glass of schnapps. "To my little sister and my brand new brother-in-law. George Bernard Shaw said, 'It's a woman's business to get married as soon as she can, and a man's business to keep unmarried as long as he can.' Walter, you never had a chance. More power to you Molly, and may the two of you bring forth a passel of kids as soon as this war is over."

Molly and Walter faced each other, holding hands. Leah took a small sharp breath. The freshness of their love was almost too painful to see.

After all the guests had gone, Harry and Ben started to clear the table. The driver had arrived, and Phil carried the suitcases down. Walter had his khaki army coat on. He held Molly's jacket as he talked with his mother.

Leah, her eyes brimming, took Molly's arm and steered her to a corner of the room. "Molly, we should have talked yesterday." She searched for words. "You're a married woman now. We should have talked." She stroked her daughter's cheek. "It's too late now to ask you if there's anything you want to know."

Molly clasped her mother in a tight hug. "I know everything I need to know, Mama," she said. "I know everything, even the things you were afraid to tell me." She gave Leah a bright smile and an upward lift of her chin.

Walter helped Molly into her jacket. Leah stood in the doorway and listened to their footsteps as they hurried down the stairs.

A DISTANT PLACE

Charlotte began haunting the mailbox in the lobby of her building long before the possibility of receiving a letter from Cairo. For two weeks there had been no letter, but her trips to the mailbox afforded her an invincible connection across the ocean to Ahmed Kamil. A letter came at last.

Charlotte clutched the letter to her breast and hurried up to her apartment. In her bedroom, she closed the door, and lay back on her pillow. She did not open the letter at once, preferring to defer her pleasure, all the more to enjoy it. She looked up at the ceiling and thanked providence for the unexpected airplane stopover in Alexandria just a few weeks before. Had it not been for that occurrence, she and her mother might never have met Ahmed. But, their flight across the Mediterranean was diverted just one hour away from Cairo for an urgent mechanical repair. They set down in Alexandria at three in the afternoon.

The passengers were guided into a narrow lobby of the terminal where they were informed that the repair would take five to six hours. They were directed to the airport lounge to wait.

Charlotte and her mother, Gladys, settled in the hard plastic seats. Charlotte's eyes scanned the passengers, some of whom she recognized as having been on the plane. One was a man in a gray business suit who stood against a wall speaking into a courtesy telephone. He ended his conversation, came toward them, and took a seat facing them.

Charlotte's mother twisted in her chair. "God knows how long we'll be stuck here." She fanned her face with a limp handkerchief.

"Just try to relax, Mother. There's nothing we can do about it."

Charlotte's gaze settled on the man across the aisle because he was staring at her. She looked away. She was well aware of her blue-eyed blonde good looks, and thought it might be fun to flirt with him. She met his gaze again and delivered a brief half-smile.

"You were on our flight, weren't you?" she said to him.

"Yes, I remember passing your seat. It's a shame we had to be diverted like this."

Gladys stood up. "I'm going to look for a water fountain," she said to Charlotte.

Charlotte tilted her head toward her mother as she hurried away. "My mother's really upset. This long wait will be difficult for her."

"I can well imagine," the man said. "I am not going to wait for the plane. I intend to take a train to Cairo."

"That's a good idea. How are you going to manage that?"

Gladys returned and sat down. She looked from her daughter to the man across the aisle.

"I am waiting for an airport attendant I know," he said. "He might be able to make the arrangements for me." He smiled at the older woman. "Are you ladies vacationing in Egypt?"

"Yes," Gladys said. "My daughter will be starting her last year at Columbia University in New York when we get back. This trip is a little treat before her senior year. Do you live here in Egypt?"

"Yes. I have just spent a few days in Venice purchasing for my shop in Cairo.

"What kind of shop do you have?" Charlotte said.

"Antiques and oriental rugs."

"Rugs?" Gladys said. "We were shopping for a Persian rug in New York before we came on this trip."

"Oh…Perhaps you would like to visit my shop while you are in Cairo. We have a large selection of rugs, and we ship all over the world."

"Maybe," Gladys said.

"My name is Ahmed Kamil. Here is my card."

"I'm Gladys Wells. This is my daughter, Charlotte.

"Charmed," he said.

Charlotte observed Kamil as he lit a cigarette taken from a slim silver case. God, how handsome he is, she thought. He appeared to be about twenty-five. She noted a diamond ring and gold cufflinks. His eyes were dark and sensuous, the richness of his voice enhanced by an elegant British accent. He was of medium build, not tall, but he possessed an enigmatic element of stature.

An airport attendant in a faded blue uniform approached.

"Ah, Yusef," Kamil said. The two men talked in Arabic. Then Kamil turned to the women.

"He says he will be able to get me on the Alexandria-Cairo Rapide. It will bring me to Cairo before our dysfunctional plane is ready to take off…Perhaps you would like to take the train. Shall I ask him to try to get two more passes for you?"

The women looked at each other. "That sounds like a wonderful idea," Charlotte said.

Gladys frowned. "I don't know. What about our luggage?"

"It would be waiting for us at the station before the train leaves for Cairo," Kamil said. Before waiting for an answer, Kamil spoke again to the attendant. "He says he can try to get two more passes."

"Wonderful," Gladys said. "How nice of you to do this for us."

"Not at all. It is my pleasure." He wrote the women's names on a slip of paper, and the attendant headed back through the terminal. In ten minutes, the attendant returned and handed Kamil an envelope. "It's all settled. I have three passes for the train,"

Kamil said. He gave a few Egyptian pounds to the attendant who bowed to the ladies and left.

"We have an hour and a half before the train leaves," Kamil said. "Perhaps we should look for some refreshments outside."

The Alexandria streets were a vortex of colors and sounds—some men in western suits, some in Bedouin robes, women in black veils over shapeless long gowns, some wearing printed western style dresses. Children surrounded Kamil, tugging at his jacket. "*Baksheesh, baksheesh,*" they called. The air, thick with heat and dust from the streets, pressed onto their faces and under their collars. Rotting garbage from the curbs sent waves of rancid odors up to mix with the smell of roasting lamb from an open stall. A lineup of customers at the stall took the food on sheets of paper out onto the streets.

They found a sidewalk cafe and ordered Turkish coffee and sweet cakes. A boy in filthy pajamas stopped at their table and held out his hand. A small monkey, tethered by a long rope around its neck, sat on the boy's shoulder. In an instant, the monkey hopped onto the table and up onto Gladys' shoulder, knocking her hat to the ground. Kamil gave the boy a coin. He disappeared with his pet into the crowd.

Kamil retrieved the hat. Perspiration beaded on Gladys' face. She wet her handkerchief in a glass of water and swabbed her forehead.

"Are you all right, Mrs. Wells?" Kamil said. "You look ill."

"It's just the heat and all the confusion. A bath and a nice clean bed is all I need. By the way, please call me Gladys. I don't think we need to be formal after all you've done for us."

"Ahmed," Kamil said, with a slight bow. "By the way, what is your hotel in Cairo?"

"It's the Nile Cairo Hilton. I hope they hold our room."

"What luck," he said. "The Hilton is just a few blocks from my flat. And my shop is close by, too. I'll call ahead to ensure your reservation." A lift of his chin brought the waiter who directed him to the telephone inside.

"Your reservation is confirmed," he said when he returned. "In about four hours you can have your bath."

After a short ride in a battered taxi, they arrived at the depot and boarded the train. They were seated in a clean air-conditioned compartment where a waiter in a white coat appeared and served them a supper of boiled eggs, stuffed fig leaves, and flat bread. As the train rolled along the Nile Delta, Gladys and Ahmed had an animated discussion about oriental rugs. Charlotte stared out the window and fantasized about a potential romance between herself and Ahmed Kamil.

At the hotel, Ahmed attended to their registration and walked with them to the elevator.

"How can we ever thank you?" Gladys said. "What would we have done without your help?"

"Not at all," he said. "Tomorrow, I must go to my shop in the morning. If you have no plans, you might want to join me. You can look at our rugs. If you wish, I would be happy to take you to see the Pyramids in the afternoon."

Gladys smiled. "That sounds like a fine idea. Thank you."

"I'll phone you in the morning."

The room reflected the exotic touches of Egyptian culture, the bedspreads quilted in fine white cotton. A double layer of soft sheer curtains hung at the windows. Soapstone statuary— an elegant ibis, a jeweled scarab, and a bust of Queen Nefertiti stood on the table tops.

A Nubian bellboy in a cotton tunic, appeared. He adjusted a calendar on the desk to the current date, August 2, 1968, turned on the air-conditioner, folded the bedspreads down, and left. A few minutes later, he returned with a pitcher of ice-water.

Gladys rummaged through her handbag. "You should have had your pill an hour ago," she said. She placed the bottle of tablets and a glass of water on the night table next to Charlotte and went into the bathroom to run water in the tub.

Charlotte undressed down to her underwear, lay on the bed, and looked up at the ceiling. The grayish paint in the plaster made a pattern of erratic rivulets. As she stared, the rivulets seemed to move, and the ceiling began to roll like a wind-driven lake. Her heart gave a wrenching throb, and she jerked her body on its side. With the vision of the undulating ceiling still in her eyes, she reached for the pill bottle. She swallowed a tablet with a gulp of water and turned face down on the pillow, clutching the bedspread. The bedspread gave way like water, and she struggled to find something solid to hold on to. "Mama!" she called, but there was no sound. Darkness drifted over her.

She awoke to her mother's frantic urging. "Charlotte, what's the matter? Get up. You're covered with perspiration." She mopped Charlotte's face with a towel. "What is it? You were thrashing about."

Charlotte sat up and looked around the room. She swung her legs over the side of the bed and hunched into herself, looking down at the floor

"You've had another episode, haven't you?" Gladys said.

"I'm all right."

"Look, Charlotte. I think we should go home. This is all my fault. It was too long a trip for you. We can probably get a flight home tomorrow."

"Why? I'm just beginning to enjoy myself. We have another week."

"You need to see Dr. Royce. He said if you have another attack, you should see him immediately."

"I'm all right, I tell you. There's nothing wrong. You're the one who's making me sick. I'm just tired. I want to sleep now. Leave me alone."

"All right. Calm yourself, dear. We'll talk about it in the morning."

But in the morning, Charlotte's attitude was combative, her voice firm with an underlying admonition that denied discussion.

When Ahmed called at nine o'clock, Charlotte picked up the phone.

"How was the night?" he said. "Did you both sleep well?"

"Yes. As you know, we were exhausted, but the hotel is quite comfortable. We've just had a lovely breakfast."

"Are you still interested in seeing my shop and the Pyramids in the afternoon?"

"Yes, we'd love to come." She looked at her mother who was fidgeting with some clothes in a drawer and did not raise her head.

"Very well. I'll meet you in the lobby in half an hour."

Charlotte replaced the receiver and turned to her mother. "All right, Mother, what's the matter?"

"Do you think you should have such an active day so soon? You need your rest, Charlotte."

"Mother, I'm not going to let you spoil this for me. You can't bear to see me happy. Stay here if you want to, but I'm going with Ahmed."

"I won't let you go alone. Yesterday, you almost…"

"Oh, stop fussing over me…stop fussing!"

They dressed in comfortable skirts and sandals and straw hats.

Ahmed arrived in the Hilton lobby wearing a sport shirt and cotton slacks. They walked several blocks to the heart of the business section. In Ahmed's cluttered shop, the pungent scent of incense hung in the air. Jamal, Ahmed's assistant, greeted them at the door. Ahmed spent a few minutes discussing business with Jamal while Charlotte and Gladys browsed among the showcases of antique jewelry and bric-a-brac that lined both walls and ran down a center aisle. They wandered to the rear of the shop where piles of small rugs lay in stacks on low tables.

A dozen room-size carpets hung from the ceiling. Gladys was fingering an exotic blue Persian rug when Ahmed joined them.

"You are looking at the most costly rug in the shop," Ahmed said.

"Oh? I sure know how to pick them," Gladys said. "How much is it?"

"In American dollars, about eighteen thousand."

"It's really something," Charlotte said, stroking the rug. "Can we get it?"

"Maybe," Gladys said. "It's truly magnificent. We never saw anything like it in the States." She turned to Ahmed. "I'd have to check with my accountant in New York. If I do buy this carpet, when can it be delivered?"

"Let's go to my desk. I'll give you the details."

Gladys and Ahmed talked for a few minutes at his desk and then went to look for Charlotte who had wandered through the narrow aisles of the shop. She had stopped before a set of antique crystal inkwells on an ornate brass stand.

"Do you like them?" Ahmed said.

"They're lovely."

"You must have them, Charlotte, as a remembrance." He removed them from the showcase. He then drew a strand of brilliant beads from a rack and placed them around Gladys' neck. "These suit you beautifully. They're my gift to you, Gladys."

Gladys fingered the beads. "They're beautiful, Ahmed. Thank you."

"Now, about the Pyramids," Ahmed said. "I'm glad to see you are wearing hats. You will need them."

Outside, they took a taxi and rode for six miles to a dirt road access leading to the plateau of the pyramids.

Approaching the plateau on foot, Charlotte saw the heat rising up off the dusty plain. They stood before the majestic Cheops. Charlotte felt a wave of nausea. Her ears blocked all sound. The pyramid in the shimmering heat waves loomed like a breathing monster. She swayed and grasped her mother's arm. A minute later, Ahmed's voice emerged bringing her back as he described the innards of the pyramids, the tunnel-like passages, the hieroglyphics.

The women declined Ahmed's invitation to enter one of the pyramids. Instead, they turned their attention to a row of vendors peddling trinkets from wooden stands and straw mats on the ground. Ahmed helped Charlotte bargain for a long black fellahin dress. A man selling red fezzes cupped into each other on a stick circulated among the sightseers. Lemonade vendors did a brisk business, and camel rides were a busy attraction.

Late in the afternoon, they stopped at a cafe and had lamb sandwiches and mint tea. At the register, Ahmed read an advertisement on the wall printed in Arabic. The ad depicted an exotic woman in a sensuous dancing pose.

"That's interesting," he said. "There is a troupe of dancers performing tonight at the Djamma Club." He turned to Charlotte and Gladys. "How would you like to go this evening? Gladys, you can wear your new beads."

Gladys shook her head. "You're so kind, but I'm exhausted. I must beg off. Charlotte should get some rest, too. Maybe we can go another day."

"The advertisement says this is the last night for the performance," he said.

Gladys shook her head again. "If you'd get us to our hotel, I'll collapse as soon as I see my bed."

"Mother, I'd like to go with Ahmed." A cold look passed between the women.

"All right...but I won't join you," Gladys said. "You understand, don't you Ahmed?"

"Of course. I'll take good care of your little girl. Don't you worry. I'll bring her home early. Tomorrow, I am off to visit my family at our homestead."

In their room at the Hilton, Charlotte washed her face and changed her clothes. At the door, Gladys handed her a bottle of pills.

Charlotte and Ahmed sat at a table for two in the night-club and sipped peppermint tea. The room was crowded with young foreign couples and groups of dark-skinned men in western business suits.

The music started with a clanging vibration and the lights dimmed. A lone dancer appeared wearing diaphanous, low-slung trousers and a tasseled bra. She started to move in slow gyrations, increasing her tempo to the music. The beat accelerated, and the dancer rolled her body in exquisite subtlety. Several other dancers joined her in mounting stages of sensuality.

Charlotte's lips parted and her breath caught in her throat. She looked at Ahmed whose gaze was fixed on her. His hand rested on the table. She longed to cover it with her own but felt daunted by his unwavering reserve. His restraint was a cultural thing, she told herself, satisfied with that for the time being.

In the taxi riding back to the hotel, they sat close, shoulders touching. At her door in the hallway of the Hilton, he took her hand and touched his lips to her fingers. Neither of them said "Goodnight" as she slipped into her room.

The next morning, Gladys and Charlotte were about to go down to the dining room when their phone rang. Charlotte answered.

"Oh, good," Ahmed said. "I'm glad I caught you. I have an idea. I would so like you to go back to your country with a feel for the real Egypt. I am hoping you and your mother will come with me today to my home in the country. You'll meet my family, and I can promise you an usual experience. What do you say?"

"I would love to come, but I don't know if my mother would agree."

"Let me speak with her."

Gladys took the phone. "Good morning, Ahmed." After a minute, Gladys said, "Where does your family live?"

"They live on the outskirts of a town called Sanhur, about fifty kilometers from here. They own twenty acres of farmland."

"I don't know…it might be an imposition," Gladys said with an anxious glance at Charlotte, who returned an exasperated message with her eyes.

"Not at all," Ahmed said. "My father is out of town, but I've talked with my mother. She would be delighted to have your company. She invites you to stay the night…Look why don't you think about it. I must spend an hour in my shop. I'll call you from there."

Gladys faced her daughter. "This is madness, Charlotte. Don't you see what's happening here? He is playing us for all our worth. He thinks I am going to buy that rug, and that's all he wants from us."

"That's not true. You don't know him. He really cares for me. Last night…he was very sweet."

"Don't be ridiculous, Charlotte. I'm not going to let you make a fool of yourself."

"Well, you can stay here, if you want to. I'm going with Ahmed."

"I'll not let you go by yourself. How would that look? And, anyway, you might have another attack. What would you do then?"

Charlotte set her shoulders in a way that Gladys knew was an insurmountable statement.

When Ahmed called an hour later, Charlotte told Ahmed they accepted.

"Very well," Ahmed said, with obvious pleasure. "Dress comfortably. Don't forget your hats. I'll pick you up in thirty minutes."

The taxi was a tinny machine driven by a brown-skinned man in a Donald Duck tee shirt. They rattled over rocks and clumps of dried dirt, passing sand dunes and mud huts. Soon, sporadic shrubs appeared, and green fields spread before them on both sides of the road. They rode through small towns, the houses made of stone with wooden roofs. When the paved road ended, they said good-bye to the taxi driver.

They walked across a stone bridge and came to a high gray brick wall divided by a wrought iron gate. Ahmed pulled a thick rope at the gate that released a latch. He swung the gate open. They stepped across an open courtyard toward a white stucco house.

A woman wearing a long black dress, and a black scarf tied under her chin, rushed out, several strings of colored beads swinging on her chest. Ahmed lifted her off the ground in a hug. A bright paisley design covered her cheeks. She flashed a smile of even white teeth as she murmured a greeting to the two women in Arabic.

"My mother," Ahmed explained with a glance at his guests. "She speaks no English, but she welcomes you to our home. Let us go inside. I know you are both exhausted."

His arm was around his mother as they approached the porch. "My mother is Moroccan by birth," he explained. "The tattoos on her face are common among the sheepherding families in the province where she grew up."

They crossed the porch and entered a large square room where a fan rattled overhead. Rush mats lay on the stone floors and a modern electric stove stood next to the fireplace. A stack of sugar cane leaned against the wall.

At a low round table, a young woman in a white gown and head scarf held a sleeping infant. She came to greet Ahmed and the guests.

"My sister, Ghadeer," Ahmed said. "Ghadeer's husband is the overseer of our family fruit farm."

"Welcome to our house," Ghadeer said in perfect English. She placed the baby in a cradle on the floor.

"Come," Ghadeer said. "I will get you settled." She showed the two women to a small mud structure twenty feet behind the house, sheltered by a palm tree and surrounded by shrubs. "We have no plumbing here," she said, blushing, as she opened the door for them, revealing a round circle cut in a solid bench.

After they washed their hands from a ladle that hung from a huge jug near the hut, Ghadeer led them to a small room at the back of the house and explained that their beds were padded mats on the floor. There was an alcove with shelves where they put their overnight cases. A small mirror was fastened to the wall, and except for a straw chest for blankets and a table holding a clay ewer of water, there was no other furniture in the room. They came to sit in the kitchen where preparations for a meal got under way. Ghadeer's husband, a dark, wiry man, joined them.

Ahmed spoke at length with his mother, translating bits of the conversation to his guests. Charlotte watched them, feeling an odd sense of pique at Ahmed's obvious affection for his mother.

After a meal of roasted pigeons with vegetables and grains, Ghadeer filled bowls of water from a hand pump outside and passed them around for washing.

The sun had shifted and darkness descended.

"Let's get some air," Ahmed said to his guests. "It is cool outside. You might need to wear a light wrap."

Two carbide lamps hanging from posts lit the porch. Gladys sat between Ahmed's mother and Ghadeer who translated their conversation.

"Come, Charlotte, I'll show you our orchard," Ahmed said. Charlotte swung a shawl over her shoulders and they walked across the courtyard. The new moon was a crescent in the black sky amid a brilliant stretch of stars. Ahmed lit the way with a flashlight down a path that led to a grove of peach trees. "Some day much of this land will be mine. My father will build a house for me right there." He directed the flashlight to a broad flat area beyond the peach trees. "I am to be married before Ramadan next year."

Charlotte wondered if he heard the thump of her heart. A few seconds passed. "Who is she?"

"Saleen is the daughter of my father's friend. She is studying now in England."

Charlotte clutched the shawl at her neck. "It must be wonderful to be in love," she said. She was aware of something akin to anger lurking under her words.

"Love?" he said. "It is not love as it is understood in the western culture. I like Saleen very much. She is very pretty. We have many things in common. In June she will have her masters degree in art history."

They started to walk back to the house, the pebbles under their feet grating on the dry earth. The friction, magnified in the stillness, sounded like crisp jets of electricity. Charlotte thought she detected a communication in the crackling—some rambling indiscernible words.

Ahmed continued. "Saleen and I have known one another since childhood. There has never been any question about our impending marriage."

"But surely you're not happy with this arrangement," Charlotte said. "Surely, you want more?"

Ahmed did not answer. He took her elbow, and they walked back across the courtyard. As they approached the porch, the red glow from the carbide lamps seemed to project a message meant for her alone. She turned to look at Ahmed's profile. She knew that somehow she would have him.

Gladys stood on the porch looking into the darkness as Charlotte and Ahmed neared the house.

"We've had a long day, Charlotte. We should go to bed." she said.

"Indeed, you must be tired," Ahmed said. "My sister will help you get ready."

Ghadeer escorted them behind the house. On the path to the mud hut, Ghadeer stopped and emitted a shrill ululating call. She continued the warbling wail as she rotated slowly in a circle. She turned to the two startled women. "It is to frighten any animals that might be lurking about," she said with a smile. "They come out at night to look for water." When they returned to the house, she filled their basins for washing.

In their room, Charlotte was aware that her mother was talking. The words oozed like molasses, emerging like the sound of a warped record. Charlotte dropped to the mat and lay like a water-logged tree. She slept.

The next day, after a breakfast of couscous and spicy eggplant, Ahmed's mother presented them with a gift of several tins of mint tea and Turkish coffee.

Ahmed accompanied them back to Cairo. Charlotte and Gladys started at once to pack for their return to the United States.

❧   ❧   ❧

෨

250 Cabrini Blvd.
New York, N. Y. 10033
September 16, 1968

Dear Ahmed,

I can't say that our flight back to New York was uneventful, because I spent the hours reliving the wonderful days we had in Cairo with you. What an exquisite adventure it was to meet your family! The three weeks my mother and I spent in Rome, Florence, and Venice are diminished by the haunting magic of Egypt. I hope to return soon.

I have filled the antique inkwells you gave me with colored inks. They're on a shelf facing a window, and when the sun shines in on them, they sparkle like jewels.

Your sister admired the scent that I wear and some of my cosmetics, and your mother was fascinated by my stretchy slippers. I have sent them a package.

It's difficult to return to the mundane activities of my life. Classes start tomorrow. One more tough year at Columbia before I graduate. The anticipation of my freedom will be a driving force—freedom to travel. I look forward to visiting Egypt again.

My mother sends her kindest regards. Please write soon. I will eagerly await your letter.

Fondly,

Charlotte

∾

Kamil & Sons
Khan al-Khalili
Sh. al-Muski, Fatimid
Cairo

October 30, 1968

My dear Charlotte,

How happy I was to receive your letter so soon after you left our country. It pleases me to know we have established such a warm friendship with you and your mother.

I have taken a teaching post at El-Azhar University. There is much opportunity for future advancement. I venture to guess that I am as nervous as my first year students are, but it is going well.

My father will take over the shop. I have told him of your mother's interest in the Persian rug. I hope she has not changed her mind. My father will be in touch with her.

Thank you for sending gifts to my mother and sister. They were delighted to receive them.

With my best wishes to you, and regards to your mother, I am,

Yours truly,

Ahmed

∾

250 Cabrini Blvd.
New York, N. Y.. 10033
November 19, 1968

My Sweet Ahmed,

Thank you for your dear letter which came this morning. I'm so glad your family received my package in good order.

How I envy the ease with which you've taken to your new job. Your students are fortunate to have such a capable and interesting teacher.

As for me, the new semester hasn't turned out as I'd hoped. My colleagues are unfriendly. My relationship with you has incited their jealousy. They whisper about me behind my back.

I live for the day when we can be together again. I have been thinking of dropping out of school—the sooner to be able to be with you.

My mother has just returned from the store. I must end this letter now. I cannot abide her interference.

Write soon—PLEASE!

Charlotte

∾

250 Cabrini Blvd.
New York, N. Y. 10033
January 10, 1969

Dear Ahmed,

I'm sure your letters to me have been intercepted. Don't worry. Fortunately, I have been receiving your loving messages through my radio. How clever you are to transmit your messages so that only I can hear them.

The situation at school is growing worse. The students in my classes are conspiring to destroy our love. I hear them whispering wherever I go. Last week they threatened me over the loudspeaker in the football stadium. Beware, my darling. Your Saleen may have something to do with it. Even my mother is suspect. She is always hovering about urging dangerous drugs on me.

You are the only one I can trust, my love. I await your letter with urgent anticipation.

Charlotte

☙

1860 Legion Street
New York, N. Y. 10545
June 5, 1974

Dear Ahmed,

I don't know how long it has been since I have written to you. I'm sure you know that I have been in the hospital. My mother passed away on April 17. Her brother, Frank, took me to the funeral and it was very sad to see her buried. But she still visits me occasionally. I believe she stays in my closet where she plays organ music at night.

Perhaps you've noticed my new address? Now that I am out of the hospital, Uncle Frank has arranged for me to live in this house with some people who have become my friends. We each have our own room and get along very well. Mrs. Herzog, who runs this place with her husband, lets me go out by myself to take the bus to my dentist. She says I can do that as long as I take my medication. Sometimes I want to kill her.

Please continue to contact me by my radio. Your messages have sustained me through my illness.

All my love,

Charlotte

∾

1860 Legion St.
New York, N. Y. 10545
September 7, 1978

Dear Ahmed,

How happy I was to see your picture in the New York Times! The article says that you are coming to New York. How modest you are! You never mentioned that you have been made the Chairman of the Committee of Egyptian Antiquities in Cairo. I envy the curator of the Brooklyn Museum who will undoubtedly see you before I will. The article in the Times says that you have deciphered some ancient writings from the museum archives. That sounds terribly important!

I haven't received an invitation to the reception in your honor at the St. George Hotel. Never mind. Perhaps it has been intercepted. I'll be there! My heart beats with anticipation.

Charlotte

❧ ❧ ❧

On a Sunday evening in September, Frank Mondale stepped out of his car in front of the Herzog residence. A man of about seventy, he was aggrieved to find himself out on this evening of his weekly poker game. But familial obligation had brought him here to drive his niece to God knows what. Mrs. Herzog, a plump fiftyish woman, let him in and invited him to sit in the parlor.

"How is she?" he asked.

"Very well, Mr. Mondale," Mrs. Herzog said. "Charlotte is very pleasant and cooperative as long as she takes her medication. I'll tell you, she's really looking forward to this outing. Where are you going?"

"To the St. George Hotel. There's a reception there for a friend she met in Egypt some years ago."

"It's almost seven o'clock. She shouldn't be out too late."

"I know, but she's so happy. She has so few pleasures these day. I'll have her home by eleven."

"I'll get her."

Mrs. Herzog almost collided with her as Charlotte bounded into the room.

"Uncle Frank. I saw you from my window. We should hurry. We don't want to be late."

He was pleased to see that she looked normal. She wore a gray suit and red blouse, and her hair was neatly combed. In the past few years, she had looked strange, her facial features askew.

There was little conversation as they drove. Charlotte was preoccupied with the contents of a quilted cotton tote bag she carried. As they approached the Brooklyn Bridge, traffic slowed, and they came to a standstill. After ten minutes, traffic started to move. "I hope we won't be late," Charlotte said. He cast an apprehensive look at her. He knew that any small anxiety could trigger an aberrant reaction. She was still rummaging in her tote bag. When she removed her hand, it was dripping something green that she wiped on the bag.

"What's that?" Mondale said.

"It's just makeup," she said. "Never mind. It's all right."

"Look, Charlotte, don't get it on the upholstery. It looks like ink."

They parked in the garage beneath the hotel. In the lobby, they were directed to the Coral Room where, in front of the closed double doors, an easel stood, holding a photo of a solemn young man and the announcement of the reception honoring Dr. Ahmed Kamil. Charlotte stood, transfixed, gazing at the photo. One of the doors opened, and a waiter came out. In the room, ten tables in a semi-circle were occupied, and a man was speaking at the dais. The waiter closed the door behind him.

"I have to go to the ladies room," Charlotte said to her uncle.

Mondale followed her as she hurried through the lobby to the restroom. He waited outside for ten minutes and then found a straight-backed velvet chair facing the restroom door. He was staring at the door when a woman stepped out. She wore a loose black gown with a sheer head scarf covering her forehead, tied in a loose knot under her chin. Her cheeks, nose, and chin were painted in a bright paisley design in red, blue, green, and black. She looked straight ahead and walked across the lobby. Mondale's eyes followed her familiar gait as she went toward the Coral Room. He rose and hurried after her, arriving just as she flung both doors open and stood in the doorway, arms outstretched. A high-pitched ululating wail rolled off her tongue and resounded in the room and out to the lobby. The man who was speaking at the dais stopped. The guests turned in their seats.

A security guard rushed in and caught her arms forcing her backward past the doors. Frank Mondale caught the look in her eyes—a look of pure rapture. Her wailing stopped as she was dragged away, struggling, past the curious loungers in the lobby.

The guard forced her into a chair near a secluded exit. Tears rolled down her cheeks in inky streams distorting the design on her face.

By the time the ambulance arrived, Charlotte had lapsed into an attitude of calm. Mondale knelt in front of her and spoke to her, but she stared at the floor. She seemed absent, as if she were in a distant place.

The ambulance carried her away. Mondale followed in his car. Poor girl. She's in another world, he thought, perhaps a better place for her.

BURNT OFFERING

Dorothy Miller entered the haven of her apartment and pressed her back against the door. She took a cleansing breath. Here she escaped the cheerful, cloying company of her coworkers at Brooklyn Women's Hospital. Here she shut out the congeniality of her neighbors, despising their chubby grandchildren and their Sunday family dinners.

Dorothy flicked on the light, hung her coat in the closet, and gave her white uniform a few superfluous tugs. She gave the room a fast survey. On the mahogany buffet stood a photograph of a fair-haired young man. The smile had a jaunty twist, the lips closed, a corner of the mouth raised. Now, when she looked into the face of her son, she took no pleasure from the smile. All she felt was fuming anger at the futility of both their lives.

At the far end of the room a bunch of artificial forget-me-nots stood in a glass vase on a table before the window. A breeze came through and lifted the thin gauze curtain. She crossed the room to shut the window and stopped. She remembered that she had closed it that morning when she left for work. Her eyes swept around the room and settled on the bedroom door. It appeared to be stirring as if it were breathing.

"David?" she said.

The door opened and her son appeared. He rushed across the room and locked the apartment door.

"David...you frightened me."

"I had to be sure you were alone," he said.

He was sweating, and the corners of his mouth turned down like those of a child about to cry. The desperation in his face did

not darken the blue of his eyes. She took in his short frame with
a glance. He had become too thin. He looked younger than his
twenty-one years.

"Are you expecting anyone?" he said.

"No. David, what is it? Where have you been? Why didn't I
hear from you?"

"Look, don't start asking questions."

"I knew you were out," she said, searching his face. "That
man Ryan called me and told me you had been released. "Three
weeks ago…three weeks," she said, her voice rising.

"I couldn't come here," he said. "I couldn't. You should've
been glad. I'm no good for anyone." He paced the room, crack-
ing his knuckles.

"Mr. Ryan called again last week asking for you. He told me
you had violated parole by not reporting to him. Couldn't you
do even that much?"

A faint stream of laughter wafted in from a neighboring tenement. Dorothy slumped down on the sofa, not looking at him,
hoping that he would come and put his arms around her. "Are
you hungry?" she said.

"I haven't eaten since yesterday."

In the kitchen, she put on a pot of coffee and fixed a platter of
ham and cheese.

"I need a beer," David said. He took one from the refrigerator
and drank from the bottle.

"What kind of trouble are you in now?" She kept her gaze on
the platter in her hand.

At the sound of passing footsteps, David looked at the apartment door and frowned. The sounds faded down the hallway.

"I need to stay here tonight. I'll be out of your hair tomorrow."

"You didn't write a line in eight months," she said. "You
couldn't write one line?" Tears welled up.

"Oh, Ma, stop it! You didn't really want my letters."

"What do you mean, David? For God's sake, what do you mean?"

"What if the mailman told the neighbors? You didn't tell them that your darling son was in the can, did you...did you?"

"No, of course not. Why should I? It's none of their business."

"Where did you say I was? On a charity mission for the church?" He snickered.

"David, how can you be so cruel after you've made me suffer so much?" She dabbed at her eyes with a tissue.

"Turn off the tears...Mother...we both know what a martyr you are."

"How can you say such things?" she whimpered. "I worried so, all alone here with nothing else to think about. There was no one to talk to. Nobody cared about me."

He glared at her, his eyes red-rimmed. He poured himself a cup of coffee.

Dorothy examined him as he sat hunched over his food. She did not recognize the brown zippered jacket that he had hung over the back of a chair. His pale hair was overgrown and spread in a soft fringe across the back of his neck. There was something vaguely reminiscent about the shape of his head although he had none of his father's characteristics.

Paul had been a squat balding man with plump fingers and a heaving chest. Dorothy recalled their first meeting. He was forty-six and she thirty-four when he was presented to her by a friend with a matriarchal concern for all the spinsters and bachelors of the world. Sylvia and Al Chapman invited them both to dinner at their small flat. On that first evening, Dorothy knew Paul took it for granted they would marry.

Talk at the table was about the weather, the neighborhood, the subway system. During a pause in the conversation, Paul suddenly announced, "I make a good living. A wife of mine wouldn't want for anything." He looked across the table at Dorothy. "I wouldn't expect a wife of mine to work."

Dorothy looked down at her food. "I guess she couldn't go to work if she had children to take care of," she mumbled.

"Hm," he said, clasping his hands across his stomach.

The possibility of marriage had taken form, and Dorothy's quiet assent made her giddy. She remembered that she had talked and laughed too much.

Their courtship in the next few weeks was swift and pragmatic with Saturday nights at the movies among hand-holding, popcorn-chewing young couples. After the movies, they had cheap Italian dinners made lamely festive with watery red wine. On a Saturday morning at City Hall, with Sylvia and Al as witnesses, they married.

Dorothy recalled their lumbering, passionless lovemaking, motivated for her by her wish to have a child and for him by obligation. They had been married so short a time, only three months before his death of a heart attack. She did not even have a photograph of her husband. She could not recall his face, and now all that remained of him was their son.

David moved from the kitchen to the living room where he seated himself before the television. He watched the screen, his feet stretched straight out and his head hunched between his shoulders as if a weight sat on top of his skull.

"How was it there?" she said.

"It was great…a real wonderland."

"Why didn't you let me visit you? I traveled three hours by bus. Three hours! And then they told me you wouldn't see me. I was so ashamed."

"Look, leave…me…alone."

They watched the TV newscast in silence. Dorothy listened with apprehension, expecting to hear her son's latest crime announced to the nation. But the newscaster bid them a cheerful goodnight, and she started to make up the sofa bed.

"Where are you going tomorrow?" she said. "What are you going to do?"

"You won't see me for a while," he said. "I don't want you to try to look for me, you understand? If you want me to, I'll call you in about a week, but don't tell anyone you saw me."

"Do you need money?"

He did not answer.

She took several bills out of her purse and stuffed them in his shirt pocket.

In her bed that night she reviewed the litany of her sacrifices—the years she had worked caring for her son, providing everything other children had—everything necessary for him to grow up decent. She had nurtured him like a new plant, watched him with pride and satisfaction as he thrived on her efforts. He had been strong like a young tree, budding with possibility. Now it should be her time to taste the good fruit. What had gone wrong?

"I did too much for him," she said aloud. The words emerged amplified in the quiet bedroom. She turned over as if to stifle them, afraid that he might have heard. He never appreciated anything, she thought. How many times had she dragged him up out of some mess? She had always been there for him.

Her sacrifices flew through her field of memories like meteors, bouncing in the dust—the nights she did his homework for him when he sat frustrated and irritable at his desk—and that wallet incident when Mr. Gibson came to accuse David of stealing it from his Five & Dime. She gave that Gibson man what for. The wallet was cheap junk, not worth the hullabaloo. She took the wallet from David the next day and threw it down the incinerator in the hall. And that floozy who got herself pregnant. Three hundred dollars it had cost her. And the truancy, the smoking in school, cheating on tests, picking fights.

She remembered and remembered until she felt she was smothering under the barrage of memories. She slept in a restless stupor until she was awakened by a noise. The clock on her night table said five-fifteen. She put on her robe but hesitated at the door. She stood, her ear pressed to the door, and listened as David left.

A week later, on her day off while cleaning the apartment, she found the gray paper carton wedged beneath the base of her china cabinet. She recognized it at once. David had had it with him when he spent the night with her. He forgot his clothes, she told herself. But as she struggled to dislodge the box, she realized it had been forced into that place. She wrenched the carton out and, surprised at its weight, carried it to the kitchen table. "FRUIT OF THE LOOM, SIZE 36" was printed on the label. Inside was a green metal strongbox with the lock twisted and the lid contorted. She lifted the lid.

On top of a pile of papers lay a parched and flattened corsage of what had probably been red roses and lily-of-the-valley. They were secured to the top of a yellowed white bible by a tangle of crisp and faded lavender ribbons. Beneath that was a wallet-size photo of a dark, plain, pinch-waisted girl in a suit, and standing next to her, her wavy-haired bridegroom. In her hand was the bible and corsage.

She riffled through all the papers, the throbbing of her heart rising in her throat. She closed the box hard, pressing the mutilated lid shut, and returned the strongbox to the carton, forcing it back beneath the china cabinet.

Why doesn't David call, she asked the walls. What should I do with those papers? Where did he get them? Oh, David, what have you done to me?

The next day, she stayed home, unable to go to work, too nervous to do anything but wander around the apartment and think of the strongbox beneath the china cabinet.

In the afternoon the telephone rang.

"This is Ryan," a man said. He hesitated. "David has been picked up again in connection with a burglary. He asked me to call you."

"Oh, I'm sorry," she said to the Parole Officer. "I'm sorry…"

"Well," said Ryan. "I don't know what more…"

"Mr. Ryan, it wasn't my fault. He never came home when he got out. You told me he was coming home. What could I do?"

Ryan said, "They've appointed an attorney for him. You may be able to see David tomorrow. Go down to the Precinct at nine-thirty." He was silent for a time. "There is nothing more…I'm sorry."

Early that evening, she drew out the strongbox. Locking herself in the bathroom, she sat on the edge of the bathtub and removed the papers, one by one.

There was a diploma certifying the high school graduation of Sally Gates. After she read every word of it, she struck a match, ignited the certificate and dropped it into the toilet bowl. She watched the water consume the flames and saturate the charred paper.

A fire insurance policy was folded in an envelope, and a document from the Army of the United States certifying the honorable discharge of William Kohner.

There was a fragile, folded air mail letter from England, red, white and blue stripes framing the small neat words—"My darling," it began.

She shuffled these in her trembling hands. One by one she destroyed them, watching with tear-blurred eyes as the thin flames advanced over the words and reduced the papers to black blotches.

She picked up the marriage certificate, and two birth certificates naming Ellen Sarah Kohner born April 6, 1962 and Richard Neal Kohner, born February 10, 1966. She tore them in half and lit the corners with one match. The scorched ends fluttered upward in the bowl and finally lay still on the surface of the water. The bible was next. Furiously she tore the pages out and lit them up with the brittle flowers and crisp ribbons. They fell in a soggy heap on the water.

There were more familial records. She burned them while angry tears fell down her cheeks. She flushed the bowl again and again, for some charred bits clung to the sides. A wave of nausea welled up. She leaned over and vomited into the bowl.

Minutes later, she emerged from the bathroom and sat in a living room chair awaiting the panacea of darkness. But the memory of the papers she had destroyed intruded—accusing her as if she had committed a bloody murder. She shrugged. They were only papers, she told herself—evidence against David. Tomorrow, I'll see my son, and I'll tell him what I've done for him.

BROOKLYN DAYS

The invitation arrived in a square buff-colored envelope. Inside the fold was a snapshot and a message written on ruled paper ripped from a spiral notebook. It read:

ॐ

Where have you been? It's been six years since I've heard from you. I had to do some detective work to find your new address so that I could get this invitation to you. Yes...I'm getting married! Mark's a science teacher and I'm nuts about him. I hope you can come. My brothers Daniel and Benny will be there with their wives (both fat), and my sister Florence (she married a judge!). Please say you'll come.

I found this snapshot in a shoebox of photos from the Brooklyn days. Thought you'd get a kick out of it.

Love,

Edie

The wedding of my friend Edie Gorsky was to be held on a Saturday night in October 1951.

The snapshot was dated on the back—December 1935—when Edie and I were nine. We stand on Herzl Street, smiling into posterity, arms linked, the buttons of our shabby coats straining over our bellies, cotton stockings hanging loose into grubby shoes. Part of a mini-tenement is revealed on one side, and a skinny dog, tail turned to the camera, sniffs the cracked pavement. In the background is a clouded view of Edie's father holding his hammer aloft behind the glass storefront of his shoe repair shop.

I tried to make out the features of the cobbler's face, recalling his wiry red hair, his short thin frame, and his bouncy walk that gave rise to his nickname, Springy. He took no offense at this name. "Come in, come into the store," he would say to the neighborhood children. "Springy has something for you." Usually it was a hard jelly-filled candy encased in shiny paper twisted at both ends. Sometimes it was a fresh stick of white chalk that he used to mark his clients' shoes.

The snapshot had been taken about a week before Springy was killed on a cold Friday morning. As I held the photo in my hands, the events of that day came back with disturbing clarity.

I had awakened that morning to the hissing of the radiator in my room. A drab gray light outside the window told me that it had snowed during the night. I hurried out of bed and cleared a frosty circle on the window pane. The courtyard below was covered with a thick layer of snow, and the clotheslines that stretched from my window to the flat across the courtyard, were topped with a thin coating. It was the first snow of winter.

The neighborhood was composed of several six-flat tenements and a few small stores on each block. The shoemaker's store was on the street level beneath the house where he lived. The next tenement housed Nate's butcher shop, the only kosher butcher shop for a mile around. Nate owned both buildings.

The neighbors said that Nate was rich although he was frugal. He worked his busy shop alone except for the few days before the holidays when his wife came in to help. A petite pretty woman, she wore her diamond rings in the store. Nate never hired help for the two houses he owned but would arrive on the block himself, at dawn, hatless with the collar of his mackinaw turned up, to load coal into the furnaces. He made repairs in the buildings—a plumbing leak or a broken window sash—on Sundays.

Edie and I had known each other all of our lives, our friendship bonded by proximity. We lived "across" from each other from birth. It had been my habit to call for Edie every morning for our walk to school. That day, in my wool coat, hat, and galoshes, with my books under my arm, I crossed the slickened street to Edie's house. The stairway in the dim hall smelled of ammonia and frying onions.

In the Gorskys' kitchen, I waited near the door while my friend was getting ready. Edie's teen-aged brothers, Daniel and Benny, were horsing around over the newspaper comics spread out on the enameled table, tossing bits of bread at one another. A piece of bread landed on their sister, Florence, who stood before a mirror hanging on a nail near the window. She turned and cast a menacing look at the boys.

"Cut that out, you animals. Right now!" The boys stopped their game and went back to reading the comics. Mrs. Gorsky, who was busy wiping the wooden cabinets with a torn-up undershirt, looked up but said nothing.

Florence, a sullen girl of twenty, paid homage to her face several times a day, powdering and rouging and painting her lips bright red. She was given to tantrums and kept the family intimidated, ranting if the bathroom was occupied when she wanted to bathe, or if her mother had neglected to iron a blouse she wanted to wear.

The kitchen was hot. Lena Gorsky's soup was already bubbling on the stove. Her thin hair hung limp on her stunted neck, her squat body set on bowed legs. Lena never joined the other women on the stoop in the summertime. Gossip was the stronghold of society on Herzl Street, and there were rumors that the Gorskys were "on relief" even though Springy and Florence both earned money.

There were other rumors, too. I had heard Mrs. Rubin, who lived downstairs, tell my mother that Florence and Nate, the butcher, were "going together." I knew Nate was married, and he seemed almost as old as my father.

Once my mother and I had been sitting on the stoop in front of our house when Florence came out of her building across the street. We watched her walk next door to Springy's store and talk with her father through the open door for a minute. Then she closed the door and walked toward the butcher shop. She almost stopped at one point as she looked through the butcher's storefront. Nate looked up, and their eyes met for a few seconds. Then Florence quickened her pace, and Nate's eyes followed her as she passed to the corner. "Whore," my mother mumbled.

The Gorskys' kitchen was getting hotter. Lena gave a few raspy coughs. I watched with apprehension as her coughing gradually built up from deep in her body, forcing her to double over. She continued to cough and retch, holding her apron over her mouth, until her face turned a bluish red. Then the coughing subsided, and her normal grayish color returned. Daniel and Benny appeared not to notice. They put on their lumber jackets and left for school.

"I need my gray skirt," Florence said to her mother. "It's at the cleaners." She left for work.

I recalled a day when Lena had a coughing spell in Nate's store: I was waiting for my mother, who was plucking a chicken, tossing the feathers into a large barrel. A plump cat gulped, with voracious gluttony, the chicken entrails that Nate threw into a basin on the floor. The scent of blood hung in the air. Lena had been sitting on a narrow bench waiting to be served. She started with a low cough, and hard as she tried to stifle it, the coughing built up into gurgling spasms.

Nate watched for a minute and yelled, "Dammit! Get out!" Lena hurried out, still coughing. The customers in the store avoided each other's eyes. Nate stood in his blood-smeared apron, his irritable eyes looking down over the countertop, strands of strong brown hair falling over his brow. When he was ready for his next customer, he said nothing but looked at the woman and gave a little upward snap of his chin.

When Edie was ready, she picked up her books and we ran down the hallway stairs. As we stepped out onto the icy stoop, Edie said, "I forgot my book report. I'll be right back."

"I'll wait in your father's store," I said.

A gust of sharp air cut through the glue-scented store as I opened the door. A small bunch of bells hanging on the door jangled.

"Hi, Springy," I said. "Can I wait here for Edie?"

"Sure." Springy smiled. "Sure you can wait." He waved me in with his hammer. "But first, can you do me a favor?" He gave a sharp toss of his head toward Nate's store. "Can you go to the butcher for me?" The morning ritual of the purchase of a bit of chopmeat for Springy's ancient foot-long turtle had been a source of amusement on the street. The turtle, named "Dummy", was housed in a huge fish tank on a table at the back of Springy's store. Springy gave me a nickel and two pennies. "Tell him I don't want no scraps and skin chopped in. I pay full price."

When I handed Nate the coins, I said, almost in a whisper, "He said no scraps." Nate weighed the meat on a piece of newspaper. "Tell that little Kike his turtle don't need no steaks."

"Look at this," Springy said as he poked the glob of meat. "Pieces of skin!" He dropped portions of the meat into the tank. I sat on a wobbly kitchen chair near the door and looked around. Tacked up on the walls were pictures of Joan Crawford, Jean Harlow, Robert Taylor, and Rin-Tin-Tin cut out of the Sunday rotogravure. Several calendars of years gone by displayed voluptuous "Petty Girls" in scanty costumes. A canary trilled in its cage in the storefront window.

I had never paid much attention to the cobbler's work. Now I watched with interest as Springy stood hammering on a slender iron shoe-tree, plucking from his lips an assortment of nails that he laid into a shoe with blackened leathery fingers. Then he took his place before his massive assembly-line machine that extended almost the full length of the store. Sanding wheels, brushes, and cutting blades, all attached to a common greased axle, had their functions. Springy pressed a foot lever, and the machine started to revolve with a loud squeal that shook the floor. He took the shoe and glided from one end of the machine to the other, turning and pressing it to the sanding and brushing wheels. I wrapped my scarf around my neck and opened the door, waving good-bye over the clamor.

Outside, Nate, wearing a red plaid mackinaw over his apron, was shoveling snow from the sidewalk in front of his shop, empty of customers. Edie came out of her house holding the railing as she started down the icy steps of the stoop. I heard Edie scream as she slid on the step and pitched forward, her knees landing hard on the sidewalk. She sat up and started to screech. A small circle of blood oozed through a hole in her stocking.

Springy's shop door flew open. He came out in his shirtsleeves, a hammer still in his hand. He looked at Nate and then saw Edie as she sat on the ground, crying. He walked a few steps toward her but spun around and ran toward Nate, puffing frost out of his contorted face.

"I'll get you, you son of a bitch," he yelled. "Why couldn't you clean our stoop before your own sidewalk?"

Springy, holding the hammer, threw himself at Nate who slid on the walk and fell backwards in the snow. Nate stood up, the shovel still in his hand, snow pressed on the back of his mackinaw. He raised the shovel high over his head and landed a ponderous blow on Springy's head.

Springy fell and lay motionless on the ground. Edie rose, and holding the bloodied hole in her stocking, she limped to where her father lay and dropped to the sidewalk.

Nate and I stood over them both, stunned, while an excited crowd gathered. Springy was dead. The doors of the butcher and the shoemaker were agape. Nate went into his shop and closed the door.

Mrs. Fein, who had come out of her house wearing a coat over her nightgown, cried, "I saw the whole thing from my window! Springy pushed him. Aye, Gott, Springy's dead!"

The police came, and after questioning the people who stood around, drove Nate away. His shop was closed for a week, but then he re-appeared and opened for business. The neighbors said he had been released pending an investigation, and Mrs. Fein, whose cousin was a lawyer, said Nate would get off because Springy had started the fight.

After the tragedy, Lena Gorsky appeared to shrivel up like a dead insect. She forgave her neighbors long enough to accept their gifts of food during the *Shivah* period, and then she gathered her children in a self-contained nest of bitterness.

After a week of mourning, Lena came out of the house with her two sons. They entered Springy's store and started to dismantle the big machine. Piece by piece, the three of them carried the machinery up into their small flat as the neighbors watched. Some of the people offered to help but were rebuffed by the Gorskys' cold silence. They stored the machinery parts to the ceiling in one of their two bedrooms. The neighbors said that Lena slept in that room, but during the day, the bedroom door remained closed.

Nate had watched the whole dismantling process from his doorway. He had plenty of time because he had few customers. Business had dropped, but he seemed not to care. He made no effort to conceal his observation of the Gorskys at their bitter occupation, but watched with surly attention as they went in and out carrying the paraphernalia. When the last piece was removed, the Gorskys locked the door of the shop and marched in silence into their house.

Nate stepped out of his doorway and summoned one of the older boys from the group who had watched the dismantling. He counted out twenty-five single dollars from his pocket and directed the boy to deliver them to Mrs. Gorsky. The neighbors waited until the boy returned with the money. He handed it to Nate who stared at the tenement door. He seemed not to hear as someone mumbled, "murderer...butcher."

My mother observed from our window that Florence did not walk past Nate's store again. Instead she went the opposite way, turning the corner and walking around the block to avoid him.

The women in the neighborhood took to buying their meat at another kosher market a distance away. Several of them traveled on trolley cars, twice-weekly, with their neighbors' meat orders and paper shopping bags. Nate came to his store daily but made no effort at pretense. He sat on a ledge in his window, looking out. Several times he dispatched a boy to press the money on Mrs. Gorsky. Each time, the messenger returned and handed the bills back to him.

One day, two weeks after the tragedy, Nate burst out of his store and leaving the door ajar, leaped up to the top of the Gorskys' stoop, raced through the hall and up the steps two at a time to the third floor where they lived. He pounded on the door and shrieked, "Take the money, Mrs. Gorsky! Please take it! I didn't mean it to happen! Ah, Gott, I didn't mean it! Mrs. Gorsky, PLEASE! Please take the money, Mrs. Gorsky!" He sobbed and leaned his head on the door, the bills clutched in his hand.

Lena opened the door to see tears streaming down Nate's face. "Mrs. Gorsky," he whispered. "Please!" He held out the money. When she made no move, he tried to stuff the bills into the collar of her dress, but they slid down her front to the wood floor. With her toe, she pushed them, one by one, over the threshold of the flat into the hall and closed the door.

After that Nate no longer went to the butcher shop. A man came around to collect the rent from the tenants and to fill the furnaces—and before long, two brothers took over Nate's business.

❦   ❦   ❦

I re-read the invitation. On the back of Edie's note I wrote, "Thanks for the snapshot. I sometimes think of Dummy, the turtle. Where is he now? And those Petty Girl calendars in your father's store—did you save them? I'll be at your wedding to drink a toast to you and Mark and to the bittersweet Brooklyn days.

DON BOSCO'S BOY

Milo Sweeney drove his 1966 black Chrysler onto a narrow dirt road off NY 17. After a mile he passed under a rusty wrought iron arch up a pebbled drive and pulled up to a two story white gabled hotel in need of paint. He registered at the desk in the lobby.

In his room a double bed covered with a threadbare chenille spread stood on a balding carpet. A green painted wooden kitchen chair faced the room from a corner. The bellhop placed Milo's suitcase on the floor near the "closet," a five-foot long alcove covered by a striped drapery. The bellhop pocketed the dollar that Milo gave him.

Milo showered behind a plastic curtain in the bathtub, wrapped a towel around his waist, and sat on the lumpy bed. He opened his brief case and removed a letter from Sister Catherine, a teacher at Don Bosco's Home for Boys. He read the letter once again.

❧

Dear Milo,

Here is your birth certificate and the photos that we talked about on the phone. I am mortified to have found them on the bottom of the cabinet that held your file. We don't know how this could have happened. As you know, our offices are being renovated, and we've been cleaning out the files. These items must have been on

*the floor of the cabinet for many years. Please forgive
us if this has caused you any problem.*

*I assume the boy in the snapshot is you. You cut a fine
figure in your sailor suit. It doesn't seem possible that
it has been twelve years since you left us. We still miss
you.*

Sister Catherine

The photos brought to mind a later picture of himself in the
annual record book of Don Bosco's Home for Boys when he
was about six, a skinny, ashen-faced boy with squinting, hungry
eyes. Anxiety hid behind a weak smile coaxed out for the camera.

Milo ran his thumb over the stationery logo that depicted the
patron saint of homeless boys, St. John Bosco. Milo lay back on
the bed and thought of Sister Catherine, the living personifica-
tion of the beloved Don Bosco.

The early days at the New York orphanage floated in his
memory in elusive snatches. He remembered wondering if
Sister Catherine was his real mother. Once he asked her if Father
Wilkins, the principal at Don Bosco's, was his daddy. Sister
Catherine's emphatic answer did not dispel that fancy for several
years. In time, the rigors and routines of Don Bosco's brought
him to reality.

Sister Catherine had nourished him with persistence and
kindness. When he wet his bed, a nightly occurrence until he
was ten years old, she would come each morning to whisk his
sheet off the bed and take it out of the room where he slept with
six other boys.

She attacked his stuttering with vigor until he was able to
speak with confidence. When he fell behind in his studies, she
tutored him.

By the time he graduated at eighteen, Sister Catherine had guided him toward a scholarship for pre-med studies at Ramsey University in Newark where her brother was the chief custodian. It had been her idea that her brother would give Milo a job at Ramsey. She saw to it.

She accompanied Milo via subway and the Weehawken ferry on that first day to Pat Riley's office. Riley was a large, disheveled, red-faced man with a hint of a smile in his eyes and a rancid cigar fixed in his mouth. He leaned back in his swivel chair. "How about a beer, m'boy?"

"Patrick Riley!" his sister said. "Whatever is wrong with you? I'm counting on you to look after Milo and to see to his moral as well as his physical needs."

"Ah...from what you've told me about him, I think he will look after himself. He must have what it takes to get through that stiff school of yours. He's a Don Bosco boy. He doesn't need a mother hen."

"Well, he doesn't need an irreverent old rooster either," Sister Catherine said. She stood and squeezed Milo's hand. "Come see me when you can, and God protect you from this old reprobate."

Riley showed Milo a vacant utility room in the basement furnished with a narrow bed and a small chest of drawers. "Sure, it's not the deluxe accommodations, but the room's warm and the bed's comfortable," he said, pressing his palms down on the mattress. "You can shower in the pool area. You got the library to work in, and the grub in the cafeteria's pretty good."

Milo's evening chores consisted of sweeping the hallways with a push-broom, filling the bathrooms with paper goods, and emptying the wastebaskets in the classrooms. A small stipend from Riley's budget paid for his food and some textbooks.

During the first winter recess at Christmas, Riley and his family took their vacation in Florida. Milo was alone in the building except for a crew of men who had come in to paint the classrooms and offices. Milo bought himself an electric heater and escaped the gloom of the building by spending several days in the local movie houses. When the painters had gone, Milo went into Riley's office to set the furniture back in place. Among loose papers on the desk, he found an old snapshot of Riley, his hair thicker and darker, standing before a white frame house with his arm around his blonde wife, the ever-present cigar jutting from the fork of his fingers. Kneeling in front of them was their lanky teenage son. Milo slipped the snapshot into his shirt pocket. He walked the hollow halls, the aching emptiness of them crashing under his feet. The next morning he returned the snapshot to Riley's desk.

❧   ❧   ❧

Milo fell asleep on top of the hotel bedspread and was awakened in the morning by an alarm clock radio on the night table that spewed a static drone of local news, a Bingo scandal in a church, an auto accident on Route 17, a barroom fight. He sat up and looked at his suitcase on the floor. Why did I come here? What will I find digging in the quagmire of yesterdays? What if I don't like what I find? But a flash of determination spurred him to get up and hang his clothes in the closet.

Milo placed Sister Catherine's letter back in its envelope. Then he turned his attention to the other papers in his brief case.

Milo's birth certificate gave the name and address of his mother, Mae Sweeney, her age eighteen at the time of his birth.

He fingered a 5x7 matte-finished photo of a sailor that revealed a robust handsome face under a sailor's hat tilted over one eye. Was this his father? He had a few weeks to find out before starting his new job at a Manhattan hospital. On the back of the photo was a name stamped in faded red ink, "Bronson Photos, Liberty, N. Y."

Another picture, a 3x4 glossy snapshot showed the same sailor in summer whites standing before a mesh yard fence, in his arms a small boy, about two years old, also dressed in a white sailor suit.

Milo stood up and put the papers back in his brief case, except for the birth certificate, the photo of the sailor and the snapshot, which he placed on top of the dresser.

It was eleven A.M. when he came down to the hotel desk to get directions to Bronson Photos.

Milo parked on Main where Barrett Street elbowed off and walked down the cracked pavement passing a string of attached two story wooden houses. Windows gaped in the midday heat and limp curtains hung out on the faded window frames. Among the shops on the street were a sidewalk church of an obscure denomination, a barbershop, and a storefront curtained by flowered sheets with a hand-printed cardboard sign on its door—PSYCHIC READER. CAN RESTORE LOST SEX. A few barefoot children played in front of the store.

Next door was the photography shop, "Bronson Photos—Established 1932" printed on the glass door.

A bell jingled as Milo entered. A green curtain on the doorway behind the counter stirred, and Milo knew someone was looking at him.

He examined the photographs on the walls—smiling towheads, family groups, wedding pictures. An assortment of frames lay in the grimy glass fixture beneath the counter.

A gray-haired man with a bulbous, pitted nose stepped out from behind the curtain. He scratched his arm under the sleeve of his plaid shirt.

"What can I do for you?"

"My name is Sweeney," Milo said. "I have an old photograph that was taken here in 1938. Would you be able to give me the name of the person in this picture? There's a number on the back." He put the photo on the counter.

The man turned the photo over. "Are you from the police, or somethin'?"

"No, I just want to know who this man is."

"I'm sorry. I can't help you,"

"Is your name Bronson? Are you the proprietor here?"

The man came out from behind the counter and examined Milo from head to toe. "That's not your business. You're from the police, ain't you?"

"No, I'm not from the police. I'm Dr. Milo Sweeney. Here." He removed a photo I.D. from his wallet and the snapshot. "The little boy in this snapshot is me, and I just want to know who the man is."

"Listen, I'm no snitch. I don't know him. Unless you want your picture taken, get out of my store."

The curtain behind the counter opened part way and revealed the pimpled face of a teenage boy.

"Mr. Bronson, it's nothing like that," Milo said. "I think the man is my father. I'm trying to find out what his name is." The heat in the store pressed on him. He wiped his brow with a handkerchief.

"Oh, I get it. I'm not havin' nothing to do with it. I told you I ain't no snitch."

"Look, it's really important. I'll be glad to pay—anything you want. There's a number on the back, 8469, and the year 1938. You must have records that you've kept."

"I got no records. Good-bye, Mister."

Milo took a twenty-dollar bill out of his wallet and placed it on the counter.

Bronson stared at the bill. Then he shook his head. "I said Good-bye. I ain't lookin' for no trouble."

Milo started to walk back toward Main Street with the thought that he should have offered Bronson fifty or more. While he considered his next plan of action, he became aware of somebody behind him. He turned to face the boy who had watched him from the doorway in the store.

"Wait up, Mister." The boy's pale hair stood up like the ruffled feathers of a chicken, eyes narrowed by puffed lids. He licked his flaccid mouth. "If you come back later, I'll show you somethin'."

"What are you going to show me?"

"Somethin'. If you give me the twenty dollars." He jerked his head in the direction of the store. "He goes to the track every Saturday night, so I can show you tonight."

"What's your name?"

"Grady. Are you gonna give me the twenty dollars?"

"Is Mr. Bronson your father?"

"Yeah. So, are you gonna come?"

"What time does your father go to the track?"

"Five o'clock, and he don't come home till late at night."

"If I come, what are you going to show me?"

"Somethin'. Come five-thirty. Bring the money." He turned and ran back toward the store.

Milo's next stop was the Sullivan County Office of Records, where he obtained a copy of a death certificate for Mae Sweeney who died on August 12, 1940. He made another stop at the Sullivan County Beacon. A newspaper clipping told the story. Two couples had set out in an old Ford after an evening of drinking at Sally's Bar & Grill and had a collision with a tree on a dark road. Robert Crane, Angela Rossi, Russel Wohl, and Mae Sweeney all were killed.

At five-thirty, Milo met Grady in front of the photo shop. "C'mon," the boy said. Milo followed him around the corner where they turned into a driveway that sloped downward below street level. They passed three doorways. Grady stopped at the next one.

"What is this?" Milo said.

"It's the cellar. I sleep in the other room. Shh…"

Grady unlocked the door and motioned Milo in behind him. The dark room smelled rancid. Overhead pipes wrapped in rags ran the length of the cellar. In a corner stood a cold black iron furnace, and along one wall were three tall metal shelves with odd-sized grocery cartons stacked almost to the ceiling. Lighting the way with a flashlight, Grady went to the far wall where he stationed himself before a round hole in the wall, about the size of a quarter. He looked through the hole.

"She ain't here yet," he said. "Did you bring the twenty dollars?"

"Who isn't here? Who are you looking for?"

"Costanza. From next door. From the gypsies. She fucks guys in there. I let her use my bed. She gives me a dollar. Wait'll you see!"

"Is that what you wanted to show me?"

"Wait a minute. I think they're coming in."

The faint sound of a door closing and muffled voices came through the thin wall. Grady pressed his eye to the hole. He motioned Milo to another hole in the wall two feet away and turned back to his place.

Milo took the flashlight from Grady's hand and aimed the beam on the cartons along the wall. He pulled one carton out of the shelf at waist height and saw a hodgepodge of photos, receipts, bills and correspondence, most of them dated 1953 and 1954. Another carton above held materials dated a few years later. He stood back a few feet to survey the potential.

Across the floor sat an empty, rusty, metal trunk. He started to slide the trunk across the floor. Grady turned from the wall with a loud "Ssh!" and then turned back to the hole. Milo lifted the trunk from the floor, placed it before the wall of cartons, and climbed on top.

He calculated the approximate location of materials dated 1938 and tucked the flashlight under his chin. After several unfortunate guesses, he found the carton. He tugged at it until it came halfway out. There it was—a manila file numbered 8469. He pulled the file out of the box and dropped it on the floor.

"Shh!" Grady looked up. His hand clutched the mound in his crotch. "Hey, what are you doin'?" he whispered. "I thought you came to see Costanza."

Milo handed Grady the twenty-dollar bill and left.

In his car, he opened the file. "Girard McTavish" was scrawled across the top of a receipt along with a faded proof of the photo—no address on the receipt—just the date and some code numbers. Milo ran his finger over the proof. Who are you, Girard McTavish? Where are you?

He bought a newspaper and went back to the hotel.

The next morning, Milo came down to the desk where Mrs. Mayer, the proprietor, and Betty, her teenage daughter sat at a table behind the counter drinking coffee. "Good morning," Mrs. Mayer called. "Breakfast is being served now. Go in and take a seat."

Milo glanced into the dining room. The din of clattering dishes and the smell of coffee wafted into the lobby. He needed a cup of coffee, but was not ready to explore the hotel's cuisine.

"Mrs. Mayer, could I speak to you for a moment?" She joined him at the counter. "Do you know a man named Girard McTavish?" Mrs. Mayer shook her head. "I don't think so. Who is he?"

"I'm trying to locate him. He lived in Liberty about thirty years ago."

"Well, I was born in this town sixty years ago. I don't remember that name."

Milo slid the photo over to her. "This is what he looked like around that time. Does it ring a bell?"

Mrs. Mayer looked at the photo for a full minute. "He looks familiar, but…"

"Let me see," Betty said. She joined her mother at the counter. "What was the name again?"

"Girard McTavish. Do you know him?"

Betty stared at the photo. She turned to her mother and whispered something.

"Well, do you know him?" said Milo.

"Your best bet is to check with Sally Feifer," Mrs. Mayer said. "She owns the Bar & Grill about a half mile out of town on 17. She knows everybody in town." Mrs. Mayer continued to stare at the photo.

"Is the bar open today...Sunday?" Milo said.

"No, but Sally lives in a flat above the bar."

"I'll try it." He picked up the photo.

On Route 17, he stopped at a diner where a hefty middle-aged waitress gave him a menu. When she returned for his order, Milo said, "Do you know a man named Girard McTavish who might be living in town? He lived here about thirty years ago."

"I don't think so," she said. She held her pencil over the pad. "What'll you have?"

She took his order and slipped the pencil into her hennaed hair. When she came back with his food, Milo handed her the photo. She held it outward and leaned back. "Well, I'll be darned," she said.

"Do you know him?"

"Maybe." She angled the photo toward the window. "It could be Old Jerry."

Milo stood up sloshing coffee onto the table. "Who's Old Jerry?"

"Well, I'm not sure. It could be Old Jerry...but I don't know. For a second it seemed to look like him...As a matter of fact," she blurted, "this sailor looks like Mae's boyfriend."

"Mae..." Milo said. "What about Mae? Did you know her?"

"Sure. Everybody knew Mae Sweeney. She lived on Webster with her grandmother. But me and my friends didn't hang around with her. She had a reputation. She's dead, y'know. But this sailor…he was her boyfriend. Could this sailor be Old Jerry?"

Milo took the photo from her hand. "Do you know where I can find him?"

She hesitated. "What do you want with him?"

"It's okay," Milo said. "I've been looking for this man because he's a relative of mine."

"Oh," she said. "Well, I'm sorry to say he's the town drunk. You can find him any day in the square near the statue." She started to write his check.

"Where does he live?"

"Try Sally's Bar & Grill. He helps her around the place when he's sober and she keeps him in booze. He sleeps in a little shack out back of her place." She gave him directions to Sally's. "Sally's probably not there now. She goes to early Mass on Sunday."

He almost passed the place—a large frame house with a wraparound porch. Over the front door was SALLY'S BAR & GRILL in neon, unlit now. The window shades in the flat above were lowered. It was only nine A.M., but Milo rang the bell. No answer.

He walked around the porch toward the back where he saw an unpainted plank wood shack that stood in an open field. Behind that was another sun-bleached structure about six feet square that looked like an outhouse. Milo vaulted over the porch rail and walked down a footpath to the shack. He knocked on the thick splintery door. There was no answer, so he turned the knob and opened the door a few inches. He heard someone snoring. He closed the door and knocked again, this time louder.

"What's that?" a gruff voice muttered. "Who's there?"

Milo took a deep breath. "Girard McTavish?" His heart thumped.

"Yeah. What do you want?"

"Can I speak to you? It's urgent."

"What the hell!" the man said. "Who are you? What do you want?"

"My name is Sweeney…Milo Sweeney." Milo stepped back a few paces. The long silence was palpable.

"Wait till I get dressed," the subdued voice said.

Milo looked up at the sky. He heard the squeak of a bed in the shack, the shuffle of feet, the scrape of a chair. What was he going to say? What would Girard McTavish say? All the questions he had held clustered in his mind now came to the surface in an impotent jumble. How meaningless these questions were—how inconsequential before the prospect of coming face to face with his father.

After five minutes the door opened. Girard McTavish stood before him, unsmiling and unrevealing. A large man with astonishing blue eyes, his face had the ruddy brown color of a man acquainted with the elements. Strands of his thick, unkempt hair lay on his forehead. After a brief intense look into Milo's face, he motioned him into the room. "I'll be right back," McTavish said. Milo watched him limp toward the outhouse dragging his left foot.

It took a few minutes to bring the dark room into focus. A narrow bed was against a wall, and a table and chair stood on the hard dirt floor under a small window. The smell of overripe fruit dominated the air. When McTavish returned, he placed the chair near the bed and sat on the mattress. Milo sat in the chair.

"Why did you come here?" McTavish said. He kept his gaze on the floor.

"You're my father."

"What do you want?"

"There are things I have to know."

"What things?"

"I want to know about my mother. I know she was killed in an auto accident."

"What difference does it make? She's dead."

"Why didn't you and she get married?"

McTavish clasped his hands in front of him. He sighed and tossed a brief glance at Milo. "You had to know Mae. She was a firefly. I couldn't catch her. She wouldn't marry me even after she got pregnant. She started running with every Tom, Dick and Harry. I joined the navy."

"How did I wind up in an orphanage?"

"Before Mae died, she and the boy lived with her grandmother…"

"The boy? You mean me."

McTavish shrugged. "Yeah. I guess so. I came back on leave a couple of times. Then the old lady died. When I came back after the war, they told me you'd been sent away."

After a long silence, Milo said, "Why didn't you come and get me?"

McTavish raised his lame foot by clutching his knee. "I was on the Tennessee at Pearl Harbor." Milo stared at the misshapen boot. "Are you satisfied now?" McTavish said. "Just leave it alone."

"But you could have come for me." Milo stood up. "Why did you leave me there?"

McTavish leaned his elbows on his knees and held his head. "The booze had me by the balls…my bum foot…I was in and out of the hospital. I couldn't take care of a little boy."

Milo's eyes stung. "Look, I can help you. I'm a doctor."

"I don't want your help. Go back to where you came from. I don't need your help."

"What about what I need? Damn it, don't turn me away."

McTavish took a bottle of whiskey out of a cupboard, and took a few long swallows. He held the bottle out. "I don't suppose you want any?"

"You don't have to live like this." Milo hesitated a beat. "I live in Manhattan. Maybe you'll want to come back with me." As soon as he said that, he realized how unrealistic it was.

McTavish's face reddened. He stared at Milo with a look akin to fear. He paced the room, his crippled foot creating an uneven shuffle on the floor. He glanced back at Milo with the expression of a trapped animal. He stopped pacing and faced his son. "I want you to leave me alone." His voice rose. "Leave this place. Don't come back here."

Milo felt himself choking on his words. "Give me a chance. I don't want anything from you—just a connection. I want to help. Your life can change now."

"You really don't understand, do you? I can't change. I don't want to change." McTavish mumbled, "I can't leave my wife."

"Your wife? What wife?"

"My wife, sonny, my wife. Here she is," he roared. "Let me introduce you!" He held the bottle high. "Isn't she beautiful?" He took another long swig of whiskey and wiped his mouth with his sleeve. He brushed past Milo with such force that Milo stumbled backward. McTavish walked out of the hut holding the bottle by its neck. Milo watched him from the doorway as he limped down the footpath. "You'll never take my wife away from me," McTavish rasped, looking back with a scowl. "You'll never take her away."

Milo raised his fist. "You've taken my life away, Girard McTavish!" he yelled. His voice wavered. "You've taken my life away."

The truth crashed down like an angry sea. Waves of his old fantasies rose. He wasn't the child of Sister Catherine or Father Wilkins. Pat Riley, that irascible good Samaritan had his own son. And Girard McTavish—he had his wife. Milo's quest was over. Don Bosco's boy—that's what he was now and forever.

PLAYING THE GAME

The beach smell awakened Francie from a chilly, aching sleep in the back seat of Mr. James' new 1932 Ford. The sharp salt air stung her nose, and the cold invaded her snug wool coat. She realized, with a start, that she was alone.

The car was at the curb of a narrow broken sidewalk that ran along a sandy field of beach grass, the feathery fronds reaching high above the car. The slender stalks extended as far along the street as she could see. On the other side of the street a few old wooden houses stood free on a dirt lot with no shrubs or gates to enclose them.

She leaned out of the car window and looked up and down the street. From a distance, her mother's high-pitched laugh and the muffled voice of Mr. James wafted through the top of the grass. She waited, her gaze fixed in the direction of the voices until she saw them approaching arm-in-arm down a makeshift path. Mr. James used his fine gray hat to fend off the dry blades that brushed against their shoulders. Slivers of straw clung to her mother's faded green coat and pillbox hat

"Oh, you're awake," her mother said. Her cheeks were pink. A hint of a smile shone in her eyes.

"Where did you go, Mama?" Francie said.

"We just stopped to stretch our legs a bit."

"Can I stretch my legs?"

"It's too late now, Francie. It's getting cold."

"You were sleeping so cozy," Mr. James said, "like a little brown rabbit. We didn't want to wake you." He reached out to chuck her under the chin, but Francie pulled back into the seat.

Francie watched them as they talked in low tones, their faces not visible from her place in the car. Mr. James brushed some straw from her mother's coat. His hands lingered on her shoulders and slid down her sleeves. A faint gray darkness rose. Mr. James opened the front door and her mother slid in. She searched in the glove compartment for a mirror and fixed her makeup.

"Why can't I stretch my legs? I want to, Mama. Why can't I?"

Mr. James turned in his seat behind the wheel. "Tell you what, sweetie. I know just the thing to make you happy. We can buy you a present. How about that?"

Francie looked at her mother.

"How about it, Marcia?" Mr. James said. "We can get something to eat and pick up something for the kid."

Her mother leaned over and uncovered the watch on his wrist. It's after seven," she said. "Well…all right."

They drove through the salt-scented streets toward the city's main thoroughfare. Francie peered out at the strange dusky avenues, and listened to the rhythmic pressure of the tires, like the pounding of the ocean in a seashell. She wished her father could have a car like this. Then they could go to Coney Island every day—she and her mother and father.

They parked on a bustling avenue where the brilliant lights from the shop windows gave a dazzle to the crowd of Saturday night strollers. Francie ran a few paces before her mother and Mr. James, who followed arm-in-arm past the shops. They looked into the window of a large luncheonette that displayed a papier-mache roast turkey. A toothless pumpkin left over from Halloween spread an impish smile.

Inside, the restaurant was over-bright, and the heat felt good. They piled their coats on the plastic seat in a booth, and Mr. James led them to the front of the store where a glass showcase displayed boxes of chocolates and a small array of toys for sale. Standing up on a shelf behind the counter was a large open box containing a set of miniature china. Pink-faced Japanese ladies strolled in exotic green and yellow gardens on the little plates. A row of tiny glistening knives, forks, and spoons arched across the top of the box like a Japanese fan.

"What would you like, Francie?" Mr. James said. "Pick out anything you want."

Francie forced her eyes away from the set of china and looked beneath the countertop. She pointed to a coloring book and crayons.

"Aw, come on, honey," Mr. James said. "You can pick out something better than that."

Her gaze flew to the china.

"Well, that's more like it. We'll take it," he told the counterman.

Francie's breath stopped in her throat, and she looked at her mother.

"Chester, you're too good," her mother said. And then, "It's all right, Francie. Mr. James wants to buy it for you."

At the table, the waiter took their orders. Mr. James opened the box of china, removed several pieces, and with thumb and forefinger, set the table, putting a little china platter and cup before each place. Then he draped a paper napkin over his arm and said, "Would you care for our blue-plate special, fried ice-cream with ketchup?" Francie allowed a bashful giggle.

He was very handsome, his hands slender and white, the fingernails shiny like those of Miss Wilson, her second grade teacher. His eyes were dark and warm as he gazed, still smiling, across the table at her mother. She recalled from the few times she had seen him that he laughed and smiled often, showing his even white teeth. It made her wonder why her papa never laughed. Mr. James always ignored her shyness.

The waiter appeared again and placed a cup of steaming hot chocolate in front of Francie with a hamburger on a roll speared with a paper parasol. Mr. James took the miniature parasol and held it over his head.

"Oh, dear," he squeaked in falsetto. "What a downpour! We'll all be drowned!"

"You're too funny, Chester," her mother said. Francie stifled a smile, and looked away. Under the table, a large brown roach crawled on the floor next to Mr. James' foot. His shoe moved and the roach darted into a seam in the floor as Mr. James put his foot over it.

The fluff of whipped cream in her hot chocolate had begun to disintegrate. She sipped some of the sweet chocolate from a teaspoon and took an apathetic bite of the hamburger. Her mother and Mr. James talked as they ate.

Francie observed her mother's profile. She looked strange somehow—younger.

The waiter appeared once more and with a flourish, handed Francie a slip of paper.

"Here's the check, young lady. Do you have any money? No? Maybe you'd better let your Daddy pay." He slid the check over to Mr. James.

Francie looked under the table again and saw that Mr. James had moved his foot. The roach was wounded, struggling in the floor seam. Francie tugged at her mother's sleeve. "Mama, I want to go home," she whispered, avoiding Mr. James' questioning eyes.

"All right, Francie."

"She's tired," her mother said with an apologetic glance across the table.

Mr. James let them out of the car a block from their house. Francie looked back and saw Mr. James watching them as they made their way through the hoary darkness of the street. Francie swung her head back, clutching her mother's arm for support and stared up at the blank sky, absorbing the unfamiliar blue-brown night, the quiet rustle of brittle leaves, and the sound of her mother's heels clicking on the pavement. They crossed to the other side of the deserted street and walked along a dingy row of uniform three-story houses, each projecting a small stoop of four steps. The darkened windows appeared to be like open, breathing mouths, imaginary sighs and secret night sounds emanating from inside. Everybody and everything seemed to be asleep. Francie shivered. The hollow sound of their footsteps emphasized their isolation. As they approached their corner, her mother's pace slackened and she began to talk in a curious congenial tone.

"You know, Francie, your father might not like it that we were out so late having a good time and all, especially since he couldn't go with us." She paused. "Maybe we should keep it a secret between you and me." Her voice was at once casual and solicitous. "What do you say, honey it could be like playing a game. We could say we went to see Aunt Elsie. You know, Papa doesn't like Aunt Elsie very much, so he wouldn't mind not coming with us." Something rattled in the box of china under her arm. "It isn't really necessary to mention Mr. James," she continued. "We could say that Aunt Elsie bought the set of dishes for you. Then maybe your father would come to like Elsie better. All right, Francie?"

Francie felt her mother's gaze on her.

"You'll be a good girl?"

The yellow glare of the street lamps illuminated the stoop of their building. They entered the dark hallway, clinging to one another, and hurried up the steps to the second floor. They stopped in front of their apartment where a slice of light came through beneath the door.

"Just a minute. Wait here," her mother whispered. She tiptoed up another flight of creaking steps to the landing that led to the roof. By a faint light through the window on the landing, Francie watched her mother remove her hat and place it in a box on the floor. Then she removed her high-heeled pumps, placed them next to the hatbox, and put on her familiar low-heeled moccasins. She descended without a sound on the stairs, and they entered the apartment.

Francie awoke to the scent of steam heat and the muffled sound of the radio from the kitchen. A man was talking about the weather. "Unseasonably cold...high winds..." he droned. She folded over to the foot of her bed and looked through the half-opened door into the kitchen, yawning and shivering in her thin nightgown.

Her mother was at the stove, her shoulders regal beneath her faded cotton flannel robe. Her hair, loosely plaited, hung down her back to her waist. Francie's father sat at the table, puffing a mottled pipe, the rough fingers of one hand buried in his dark unkempt hair.

"Is there any more coffee?" he said. Her mother hung a dish-towel over one shoulder and filled her husband's cup. She stood at the table, still holding the pot.

"Well, Jack, did you ask for the money?"

He sighed. "I did, Marcia, but he just doesn't have it. Christ, you can't get blood from a stone."

"You had no right to lend anybody money when we're so broke ourselves," she yelled. "You had no right. It's getting cold and we all need winter things." Two thick veins bulged in her neck. "You'd take the food from your own child's mouth for any bum who gives you a sob story!" She put the coffee pot on the stove. "Ha! John D. Rockefeller gives away money! Such a big business tycoon...such a financial wizard." She turned away and started to clear the table.

"Marcia, I told you why Hal needed the money. If I were out of work for three months, who would we turn to?" The radiator in the small room hissed like an evil, spiteful spectator.

Francie turned face up in the bed. A yawn hovered in the back of her throat, but she held it back, reluctant to relinquish the anesthetic half sleep. On the ceiling the brush stroke scars in the paint flowed like little rivers into each other in haphazard streams. As she stared at the ceiling, a hazy scene emerged from somewhere revealing a picture of her mother and father, smiling and talking, looking into each other's eyes, standing close, touching. But it was from another time and place.

"Come on, lazybones, get up!" her father said coming into the room. "I'm going down for the Sunday papers. Do you want to come?"

Francie rolled out of bed. "I want to come. Wait for me, Papa." She hurried into the bathroom, where she splashed some water on her face, and into the kitchen to sit at the table, her bare feet brushing the cold linoleum floor. Her mother put a bowl of oatmeal in front of her and Francie started to eat it in great gulps.

"Don't rush," her mother said. "He can wait for you. It's little enough he can do for his own child."

A strong biting breeze met them as they walked down the street. They leaned forward, pushing against the wind. Francie huddled close to her father, twisting her folded fingers into his big hand. His grasp was tight and it hurt, but she didn't mind. She pressed her cheek against his rough sleeve.

As they approached the corner, the wind hit them with a blast, and he bent to fasten her collar tighter. When her hat flew off and dropped to the sidewalk, he knelt to retrieve it. A spray of sharp dust swept up from the street and pummeled their faces. He rubbed his stinging eyes until a tear streamed down and settled on his cheek.

Francie stared at her father who was still kneeling before her. A surge of grief swept up in her throat. She wiped the tear away with her fingers and put her arms around his neck. "Papa, don't cry," she whispered. "Please don't cry." He lifted her off the ground and held her tight as they tucked their heads down together against the wind.

978-0-595-37110-5
0-595-37110-8